Other books by Raymond Bean

Sweet Farts

Sweet Farts
Rippin' It Old-School

Sweet Farts
Rippin' It Old-School

RAYMOND BEAN

PUBLISHED BY

PRODUCED BY

Text copyright © 2010, Raymond Bean
All rights reserved.
Printed in the United States of America

10 11 12 13 14 15 16 / 10 9 8 7 6 5 4 3 2 1

Published by AmazonEncore
P.O. Box 400818
Las Vegas, NV 89140

Produced by Melcher Media, Inc.
124 West 13th Street
New York, NY 10011
www.melcher.com

Library of Congress Control Number
2010907068

ISBN-13: 978-1-935597-08-7
ISBN-10: 1-935597-08-6

Cover design and illustration by Michelle Taormina
Interior illustrations by Ben Gibson
Interior design by Jessi Rymill
Author photo by D. Weaver

For Stacy, Ethan, and Chloe.
Also, for Baba, who would do anything for us.

Contents

Preface

I don't care who you are, you farted today. I know it, and you know it. Farts are the great equalizer. Kings, queens, presidents, and dictators fart. There are very few things in this life that all people have in common. We breathe, we drink, we eat, we poop, we pee, and yes . . . we fart. Anyone who tells you otherwise is not telling the truth. The sun rises every morning, the earth spins on its axis, and people fart!

In fact, most people do it twelve to eighteen times a day. That means that every day on planet Earth humans lay somewhere between *84 billion and 120 billion farts!* In number form that's 84,000,000,000–120,000,000,000 farts per day. Good luck doing the math for a week, a month, or a year.

What makes farting so unique is that it comes with a lot of rules. In many ways it is taboo. Depending on who you are and where you live in the world, farting can be a very complicated experience.

There are times in life when farting is absolutely inappropriate and unacceptable in any form. In these situations, people become shocked and offended by it, like if a person released a "beast" in the middle of a wedding ceremony! This would certainly *not* be taken well by the other people at the wedding. They would gasp in absolute shock, and the guilty party would be viewed as a monster, unfit for proper society.

For the most part, people spend their lives trying to hold in their farts. They hold them when they are in line at the bank, sitting in class, and riding in the car with friends. But when they are alone or with their inner circle, the rules change. For example, you would most likely not rip one off standing in line at the public library. If one slipped out at the library and everyone heard, you would probably feel embarrassed, and people would give you The Look. You know The Look. You have gotten and given The Look. It is the how-dare-you-do-that, shame-filled glare that people direct toward someone they feel has farted at an inappropriate time.

If, however, after checking out your books and getting in the car, you find yourself sitting next to your sister or brother, the rules change again. You might pull the cord and laugh yourself silly as your sibling suffers at the losing end of your stench.

Farts have rules, lots of rules. I have worked hard and spent many an hour attempting to compile a thorough list of the complex laws that govern the world of farting:

List 1: When It Is Socially Acceptable to Fart
1. When you are alone.

That's it! You may only fart when you are alone. The world does not bend on this rule.

List 2: When It Is Not Socially Acceptable to Fart
1. Any time another human is with or near you.

It turns out, the laws of farting, although seemingly complex and hard to understand, come down to these two simple rules: Fart when you are alone, and don't fart when around others. It seems so easy. The problem is that many people do not respect these laws. They spend their lives farting whenever and wherever they please. They drop the bomb in the classroom, they pop the bubble in the restaurant, they snap one off the bus seat on the way to school in the morning. They are the problem, and the question I must ask of you is this: Are you one of them?

CHAPTER 1

They Call Me Farts

"You guys seriously need to stop calling me S.B.D.," I said to Scott and Anthony. We were waiting in the lobby of the WRSEC radio station. I was pacing back and forth and biting my knuckle.

"Keith, don't be ridiculous," Anthony replied sarcastically. Anthony had been blaming me for his farts at school since fourth grade. "Your name is S.B.D. because you've earned it. You rip farts that are both silent and deadly. You didn't drop all those horrific farts in class last year for nothing, did you?" He was laughing as he spoke because he loved the fact that I had taken the blame for his school farting all this time.

"Okay, you seriously have to not call me

S.B.D. anymore," I demanded. "I'm about to do interviews in a few minutes with reporters from all over the world." I spoke in a low voice. Anne, the woman from the radio station, was standing only a few feet away.

"Okay," Scott replied, laughing, "we won't call you S.B.D. anymore. Is that what you want to hear? How about we call you Sweet Farts?"

"Awesome idea," Anthony said, nodding.

"Shhh!" I held my pointer finger to my mouth. "No, that is not an awesome idea."

Anthony and Scott were giggling when Anne approached. She had on a headset and held a clipboard in her right hand. "Are you ready to do this, S.B.D.—sorry, I mean Keith?" She started walking down the hall and motioned for me to follow.

"I think so," I said. I looked over my shoulder at Scott and Anthony, who were walking behind me, still laughing. They were making ridiculous faces at me and trying to make me laugh. *It must be nice to be so silly all the time,* I thought. *These guys get to goof around all the time, and I have to be all serious and take care of business.*

We reached the door at the end of the hallway. Anne stopped at the door with her hand on the knob and smiled a reassuring smile. "Are you sure you're ready for this?" she asked one last time. "This will be just like we talked about on the phone. You will do about thirty interviews, one after the other. Once you get through the first interview you should be fine. The reporters will be asking you about your success after inventing Sweet Farts."

"I guess," I replied weakly.

"You guess? You had better do more than guess, Keith. These reporters are going to ask you a lot of questions, and you had better be ready. Just stay focused, and think before you speak. We're going to go in and sit at that desk." She pointed through a window in the door. "I'll be sitting right there next to you if you need me. Put on the headset on the desk after you sit down, and you will be linked up to your first interview. You will be interviewed by one person after another. If you have trouble understanding any of the questions I'll be right there to help. Are you sure you're ready?"

I took a deep breath. "I'm ready."

"You're going to do great," Scott blurted out as he slapped me on the back. He winked at me and smiled.

"You're probably going to mess the whole thing up, S.B.D," Anthony said with a very serious face while looking me right in the eyes.

"Why do you have to do that?" I asked. "I'm nice enough to take you here and this is the thanks I get?"

"Sorry, Keith. Let me try again. You are going to completely"—he paused between each word to really make his point—"mess . . . this . . . thing . . . up! What I mean is, you're not going to do well." He was smiling a huge sarcastic smile.

"Don't tell the guy that," Scott said.

I just shook my head in disbelief. Why had I brought Anthony here? I shouldn't have been surprised, but I was.

"We need to go now," Anne insisted.

She opened the door, and I noticed that my palms were sweating like crazy. I rubbed them on my jeans as I walked in. Anne walked ahead of me. She sat at the desk and motioned for me to sit next to her. The whole thing was happening in slow motion. Was I ready for this? Was I ready to interview with reporters from all around the world? I was about to find out.

Anne handed me a headset as I sat down. I put the headset on and immediately heard the voice of a woman. "Hello from Italy," she said, with a faint Italian accent. "Before we start, I would like to personally thank you for inventing Sweet Farts. I must admit that I have a brother who farts so bad I sometimes want to cry. Thanks to your invention, when I see my brother, all I smell is bubble gum. I have it shipped directly to his house once a month."

"Thanks," I said. "Bubble Gum is our newest scent. I'm glad you don't have to smell your brother's farts any longer. We have a few other scents that just came out recently. We now feature Tangerine, Cookie Dough, and Blueberry."

"I'll have to go buy those and send them to my brother. Can you quickly explain how Sweet Farts works?"

"Sure, without getting into the science behind it, you eat one or two scented Sweet Farts tablets and after about ten minutes you're all set. If you have to pass gas, it will smell like the scent you ate."

"How has your life changed since you invented Sweet Farts last year?"

"Actually, my life is pretty much the same. I play on my local baseball team. I spend a lot of time with my family and friends. You know, regular kid stuff."

"Be that as it may, I think you are the only ten-year-old who has created an invention that changed the world like Sweet Farts. Can you tell me what inspired you to try and cure the smell of human gas in the first place?"

"Well, I had this problem at school. A kid named Anthony was farting every day in my fourth-grade class. He would do it really quiet and then blame it on me after everyone smelled it."

I could see him and Scott through the glass in the door. He was close enough to see me, but not close enough to hear what I was saying. He and Scott waved back at me. I waved back with a fake smile. Anthony held his nose and then pointed to me as he laughed like crazy. I knew hiring him to work with me had been a mistake. All he had done since I'd hired him was to make my life more difficult.

"I understand Benjamin Franklin wrote a letter about curing the smell of human gas back in 1781. How does it connect to your invention?" the woman asked.

"Well, when I first came up with the idea to cure farts for my science-fair project I was sent to the principal's office. Then my principal told me about a letter Franklin wrote. In the letter, Franklin wrote that if someone could cure the smell of human gas it would be the greatest scientific discovery of all time. So my principal made me do the experiment."

"I read that you had some help inventing Sweet Farts. Can you tell me a little about that?"

"Sure. I was approached by a scientist named Mr. Gonzalez. He has a scientific laboratory here in New York. He and his scientists helped me experiment and find the cure for farts."

"Do you still talk with Mr. Gonzalez?"

"Yes, he helped me set up my own company. My friends and I have a space in his laboratory for our experiments. As a matter of fact, I am meeting with him after today's interviews."

Scott and Anthony had tilted their heads to the side and closed their eyes, pretending to be asleep. *Thanks,* I thought. *I'm working hard doing these interviews, and all they can do is make fun of me.* The woman on the other end of the line asked me a few more questions and said goodbye. As I took the headset off I thought, *That wasn't so bad.*

"That was great, Keith. You seemed really comfortable. Only, try not to pay attention to your friends. They seemed to be a distraction for you."

"That's nothing new. They are always a distraction for me. It's what they do."

Anne connected the next call, and it went pretty much the same. Then it was a blur of interview after interview. They all asked pretty much the same questions—"Why did you invent Sweet Farts? How did you do it?"—and they all thanked me for fixing the smell of farts. I guess farts are a problem wherever you live. It felt good to have invented something that so many people were thankful for.

I was feeling pretty good about myself as the last interview began. It was a man from Japan. He asked the usual questions, and then he asked me something that took me by surprise: "So, the BIG question now is, what will be your next amazing invention, Mr. Silent But Deadly?"

"I . . . ummm, well," I started. The problem was that I had been thinking of about a million different ideas and really had no clear plan for my next experiment. I was really stumbling and confused. Then it happened.

Anthony opened the door to the interview room and stuck his head in. "Keith, don't worry. We're not going to call you S.B.D. anymore," he said through his laughter.

"Close that door, please. We are in an interview in here," Anne scolded.

"Sorry, I just wanted to tell Keith that we are not going to call him Sweet Farts either," Anthony added.

"Okay, thanks, but it's not really a good time, you know, Anthony!" I pointed to my headphones.

"Sorry—just wanted to let you know your new nickname from this day forth is officially Farts." Then he whispered, "Good luck with the interview, Farts."

I thought I was going to fall out of my seat. Did he really just say that? I was going to have my nickname changed from S.B.D., Silent But Deadly, to Farts?

"Did someone just say that your nickname is now Farts?" the man from Japan asked.

"Yes," I said, defeated. Through the glass I could see Anthony and Scott both holding handwritten signs that read "Hi, Farts." They were cracking up and pointing at me. "Yup," I said, shaking my head in disbelief, "it looks like they call me Farts."

CHAPTER 2
Seven Weeks

As I walked out of the radio station I felt numb. I invented Sweet Farts so I wouldn't have to deal with the nickname S.B.D. (Silent But Deadly) anymore. Now I was in an even worse situation. I was suddenly Farts Emerson! To make matters worse, I had to come up with some kind of amazing invention before the next science fair. I could feel my heart racing and my palms sweating all over again. I was walking with Anthony and Scott, and I could see they were talking to me, but I didn't hear a word they said. I was officially freaking out!

The limousine that drove all of us to the radio station was outside, waiting. The driver got out when he saw us coming and opened the door. I got in first.

"How did it go?" Mr. Gonzalez asked as he hung up his phone and put it in the inside pocket of his business suit. He was sitting across from me with his back to the driver of the limo. Anthony and Scott jumped in and sat on either side of me.

"Pretty bad," Anthony blurted out. "Farts here kind of dropped the ball."

"First of all, don't call me Farts," I said. "Second of all, I was doing pretty good in there until you came bursting into the room and announced that you were going to call me Farts. The guy from Japan heard that, you know."

"Guys!" Mr. Gonzalez interrupted. "You really need to stop acting like goofballs here and start taking this more seriously. You've had plenty of time to work on your next science-fair project, and I still haven't heard what you guys are planning to do."

"I'll figure it out, Mr. Gonzalez," I said. "I could really use a little help from you or one of your scientists, though. I am only ten years old, you know."

"Keith," he began, "we went over this already. I gave you the space at my lab for you to continue your scientific experimentation on your own. You have the help of the scientists at the lab if you need them, but the idea must come from you."

"I'm not so sure I can come up with another amazing invention," I admitted. There, I had said it. The cat was out of the bag. I was not cut out for this kind of pressure. There was no way I was going to be able to come up with something as amazing as Sweet Farts. So why even try?

"Well, you are going to have to, because you are scheduled to appear on *The Helen Winifred Show* the night of the science fair to talk about your next experiment."

"Why did you schedule that? I can't go on national TV. I'll make a fool of myself. I'll be a laughingstock. I can't do this!" I said, feeling the panic rise inside me.

"Well, you had better get busy and figure it out then, because the science fair is in exactly two months. I will be leaving tonight for a seven-week dig in Africa. I will be unreachable, but you have the full support of the lab and the scientists there. You just have to explain to them what your idea is and they will help. You also have the support of these two." He pointed to Scott and Anthony, rolling his eyes. I turned to my left and saw that Scott had been playing Jezula's Last Stand on his mobile game system. He had earphones on. Then I turned to my right and saw Anthony completely asleep. His head was tilted all the way back, and there was a little bit of drool running from his lower lip to his chin. I closed my eyes and put my head in my hands.

"Well, you're home," Mr. Gonzalez informed me. "I suggest you get that scientific mind of yours in motion. The clock is ticking, my boy. See you in seven weeks. I'll drop Video Boy and Sleeping Beauty off at their houses on my way to the airport. Good luck, and tell your parents I said hi."

The driver got out and opened the door for me. It was raining really hard.

Scott stopped playing for a minute and looked at me. "What did I miss? Where are we? When did it start raining so hard?"

"You seriously didn't hear any of that conversation the entire way home?" I asked.

"No, I was running from Jezula. Why? Was it important?"

I looked at Mr. Gonzalez in disbelief.

"*You* wanted to hire these guys," he reminded me. "I'll see you in seven weeks."

CHAPTER 3

I Didn't Mean to FAWT!

I walked slowly up the front path in the rain. It was cold and wet, but I was in no hurry to get inside. My family would be in there, probably all excited to hear how the interviews had gone. When I finally reached the front door, I slowly put the key in the knob. As I did, I could hear my sister Emma inside throwing a wild fit. She was really emotional lately and this was becoming our routine. As I opened the door I could hear my mother. She was not exactly yelling but not exactly not yelling. She was clearly angry. There was no doubt about that.

"Emma, you cannot throw your food on the floor," I heard her say as I opened the door and walked in.

"I didn't throw it on the flow," Emma began.

Even though she could pronounce her *R* sound correctly, Emma had developed a habit of not saying her *R* sound correctly. So she said *flow* instead of *floor* and *stow* instead of *store*, and it made my mom nuts. Emma didn't do it all the time, either—only when she was trying to frustrate my mom.

"Emma, it is *floor*, not *flow*. I know you can say it because I have heard you say it before," Mom said sternly.

"No, I *caaaan't*," Emma whined. She was also super whiny lately.

My dad came upstairs from the basement and walked into the living room as if nothing was going on. He waved and smiled as he walked by me and out of the room. My mother hadn't even looked at me yet, even though I was standing in the room with her and Emma.

"Hi, everyone," I announced. "The interviews went really crummy, thanks for asking. I feel like I might lose my mind if anyone cares."

"Emma. You pick that hot dog up off the floor or you are not having dessert," my mom threatened. I couldn't believe that no one had even realized that I was there.

"I don't want to pick it *uuup*! And I want *dessut*," she whimpered. Then she ripped the loudest fart you have ever heard exit the body of a four-year-old. As soon as she did it she started giggling like crazy. My mom's face went from light red and annoyed to deep red with anger instantly. She turned immediately to me.

"Are you happy, Keith? Thanks to your little invention, your sister has no control of her flatulence," Mom half-yelled.

"That one is gonna smell like cookie dough, everybody. Enjoy!" Emma announced through her laughter.

"Thanks to me?" I began. "How can you blame me for the fact that Emma can't control her farts?"

"How many times do I have to tell you that I do not like that word?" Mom began. She was now so angry I'm not sure what the proper word would be to describe it.

"Yeah, Keith," Emma began. "Mommy doesn't like the word *faaawwwwt*." She dragged the ending of the word out to really let it sink in that she was not using her *R* sound. Then she crossed her arms dramatically.

My mom hit her boiling point. "Emma, go to your room! No dessert tonight. You are going to bed. Keith, while we're at it, go to your room, too. You are going to bed as well. I am done tonight." Emma immediately fell to the floor and started crying and rolling around.

"How exactly did I get in trouble again?" I asked. "I just walked in the door! It's not even time for bed."

"Go to your room, Keith," my mom said in a very firm tone. I stormed out of the kitchen and up the stairs. I slammed my door behind me and jumped into bed. I wasn't crying, but I was close. In the distance I could hear Emma going completely ballistic in the kitchen. She was shouting, "I DIDN'T MEAN TO FAWT! I DIDN'T MEAN TO FAWT!" over and over again. Like I said earlier, I was in no hurry to get in the house.

CHAPTER 4
Fart Boy

I must have fallen asleep, because the next thing I knew I was opening my eyes and it was morning. I looked at the clock: It was eight thirty. I was still in my clothes as I sat up and stretched. I could hear Emma's favorite show on the TV downstairs and her talking dollies. I stretched again from my head to my toes. I felt a little better having had a good night's sleep.

Then my mind started going back to all the things that were going on. I had seven weeks to come up with a change-the-world science-fair project. I couldn't follow up my Sweet Farts invention with just anything. It had to be amazing and at least as good as Sweet Farts. The stress started to kick back in as I sat down at my

computer. I had loads of new emails and text messages.

I opened the first email, and it was a link to a newspaper article with the title "They Call Him Farts." I read it and checked the other emails. Each one I opened had a link to another paper with a similar title. The Japanese paper's title was "Can Farts Emerson Change the World Again?" And it had a picture of me underneath. I sat back in my chair. *How in the world had this happened,* I thought? *How did I go from just a regular kid a year ago to Fart Boy?*

I heard a car pull into our driveway and I knew it was Grandma. She was right on time, as always. I jumped out of my chair, brushed my teeth super quick, changed into my clothes, and ran downstairs. Mom was at the kitchen table on the phone. She hung up when she saw me coming.

"I'm sorry about last night," she began. "I'm just at my wits' end with your sister. She hasn't eaten a good meal in as long as I can remember, and her new hobby is passing gas as often as possible. I don't know what to do with her. I never even asked you how the interviews went last night."

"It's all right, Mom. I have to get to the lab," I told her. "Just go online and you can read the interviews from yesterday. Most of them are posted already. Let's just say you aren't going to like my new nickname! I'll see you later." I gave her a kiss and walked out the door.

I opened the door to Grandma's car and immediately heard the sound of my favorite band, Turpentine Fire Line. "Good morning, rock star," Grandma said.

I slid into the back seat of her car. My grandma still makes me sit in the back of the car even though most of my friends ride in the front.

"What's the dilly?" she inquired, looking at me in the rearview mirror.

"What's the dilly?" I started. "Oh, the usual. My friends are completely useless, my mom blames me for the fact that my four-year-old sister farts like a ninety-five-year-old man at a bean buffet, and I have to come up with an amazing science-fair project in the next seven weeks. Aside from that, everything is just awesome."

"Don't forget your new nickname, Farts!" she said, still smiling.

"Why would you say that to me? It's bad enough that I have Scott and Anthony giving me grief about it, and it seems to be all over today's newspapers."

"I think it's a fun name," my grandma continued.

"A fun name? You think it's fun to have the nickname Farts?"

"I do. I think it's fun." My grandma had a habit of always trying to find the positive side to things, even when there was no positive to be found. No matter what happens she will always find the positive in it. I love that about her, but in situations like that, it was silly. There was no fun in having the nickname Farts. She knew it, and so did I.

CHAPTER 5
That Was AWESOME!

The single greatest thing that has happened to me since inventing Sweet Farts has to be the lab. My lab is more than just a regular old science lab. It is the ultimate hangout spot. The space is awesome.

When Mr. Gonzalez gave me the space he told me I could plan it however I wanted. Sweet Farts was making a ton of money, and the lab was the only place where I was allowed to spend any of it. The rest went into a trust fund for me to use when I am older. Planning and setting up the lab was pretty much where most of my time and energy went all summer.

The first thing we did when building the lab was to put in a full basketball court. Because the ceiling was so high, it worked out perfect. We have

a real hardwood-floor court, glass backboards like
the pros, and a refrigerator full of all my favorite
drinks. We also put in a Ping-Pong table, a pool
table, and a whole bunch of video games hooked
up to a huge TV. But the crown jewel of the lab
is what is behind the lab. Out the back door of
the basketball court is a full baseball field complete
with two dugouts, a pitching machine, and a home-
run fence. I could spend all day back there hitting
off the pitching machine or playing with my dad
and some friends.

My company consisted of me, my dad, Scott,
Anthony, and Grandma. Each of us got our own
space to try and come up with ideas. We decided
that one room would be for me, one would be for
my dad, another would be for Scott and Anthony,
and the last room would be for Grandma. Each
person was free to research and think about ideas
that might help change the world for the better.
Anthony and Scott called it the Fart Factory. I
called it heaven. It was my favorite place to be. The
only problem was we still didn't have an official
company name.

Grandma and I arrived at the lab at about
9:20. The front door was already open and I figured
Scott and Anthony were there, because Dad's car

was nowhere in sight. When I walked in I expected to see Anthony and Scott playing video games or shooting baskets, but the place was dead quiet. I was amazed: Did this mean they were actually working?

"What's this all about?" Grandma asked.

"I'm not sure," I said. We walked down the hall to Anthony and Scott's lab room. As I walked up to the door I heard Anthony say, "Come on, throw up already!"

I opened the door, and the two of them were hunched over a bucket as if they were trying to puke.

"What in the world are you two doing?" Grandma blurted.

Scott took a deep breath and looked up. His face was all red from trying to throw up. "We're trying to invent something that will make people's vomit smell good. We both ate a secret blend of some of the same ingredients as Sweet Farts about an hour ago. The problem is we can't get ourselves to throw up to see if it works. We've been trying all morning."

Around the room were small glasses filled with disgusting mixtures. They must have been drinking them in hopes of getting sick.

Anthony stood up, looked right at us, and cracked a raw egg into a huge glass. Then he filled it halfway with cooking oil and topped it off with what looked like maple syrup. He then picked up the glass and started chugging. He was making all kinds of horrific gulping and gagging sounds as he tried to get it down. "Anthony, stop that this instant," Grandma said. "You are going to faint." As she spoke she gagged and looked like she might throw up, too.

Anthony kept on going. Egg was running down his chin and neck. That kid doesn't listen to anyone. He just does what he wants, when and where he pleases.

Scott shouted, "Yeah! Go! Go!" and pumped his fist in the air to cheer Anthony on.

The more Anthony kept trying to drink, the more Grandma gagged. She rushed up to him, gagging and holding her hand in front of her mouth as if she might burst.

"Anth—" she began but was interrupted by a gag. "You can't—" Another gag.

Scott and I were looking at each other and starting to laugh. Just then the door opened, and in walked my father.

Now, my father is a notorious "easy puker," as

he would put it. If he gets the slightest scent of barf, it's all over. He will throw up. As soon as he saw Anthony chugging and heard Grandma heaving and making all those guttural sounds, he pulled the trigger. He exploded all over Scott's shirt and face. Scott immediately blasted back onto Dad's chest and hands as he put them up in a failed effort to block the steady stream of mess coming out of Scott. Almost simultaneously, Grandma burst all over the side of Anthony's face and neck. Anthony, in turn, stopped drinking. Everyone just stood there staring at each other for what seemed like minutes. It was like a scene right out of a horror movie. Anthony spoke first.

"That was awesome!" he shouted.

Without warning, Grandma hurled on him one last time. After a second or two, Anthony farted, laughed to himself, and then finally puked all over Grandma's shoes.

It was indeed awesome!

CHAPTER 6

Company Meeting

After several hours of cleaning, scrubbing, and complaining, Scott and Anthony's room was finally clean, and so were they. We were all sitting around the table next to the basketball court—Dad, Grandma, Scott, Anthony, and me. It was lunchtime, but no one even mentioned food. I spoke first.

"Okay," I said, "so everyone agrees that we are not going to try and fix the smell of vomit? I think I have seen about enough of that for one lifetime." The others nodded in agreement. "Okay then, we know we will not be experimenting with barf. Other than that, do we have anything that we are working on that might actually be a good idea, because I am starting to freak out." I waited.

"I really have no ideas, you guys."

Anthony and Scott looked at each other.

Scott spoke up first. "Anthony and I are working on a little something called the Silencer."

"What is the Silencer?" I asked.

"Well, you know how some farts are really loud," Scott said.

I looked at my dad. "Yeah, I have some experience with that."

My dad made a face and said, "I can't control what your mom does, son, you know that."

"Big help, Dad. Way to contribute. Go on, Scott." I made a "give me a break" face at Dad and shook my head a little.

"Well, what if we invented something that eliminated the sound of all farts? Sweet Farts makes farts smell good, but the Silencer finishes the job by getting rid of the sound completely. What do you think?" Scott looked around for approval.

"I don't know," said Dad. "I think I would be more interested in an amplifier of some sort. You know, something that would make the sound actually louder. I know as a consumer I'd be interested in something like that."

"Do we have any ideas that don't involve

farts?" I asked. "We are able to work outside the science of farts, you know."

Grandma raised her hand.

"Grandma," I said, "you don't have to raise your hand. You can simply speak."

"First of all," she began, "I just want to say you are so cute I can hardly take it right now. You are so in charge and running the meeting. I think it's just a hoot."

"I'm very happy for you, Grandma. I assure you, though, this won't be cute anymore when everyone realizes I have no ideas in seven weeks. So please tell me you have something that does not involve farts."

"Okay," she said as she stood up and walked toward me. "I have an idea that I am really psyched up about! Picture this, fellas: You go to the supermarket, and you are shopping for fruit. You have been in the fruit aisle a million times in your life, and it's the same old stuff—apples, oranges, grapes—and then you see something you've never seen before. You see a stack, one on top of the other, of hundreds upon hundreds of square pears!"

No one said a word. I tried to think how to respond and couldn't really come up with anything. My head tilted to the side a bit and I almost said something, but certain things require no response. Silence was definitely the way to go at first. I finally broke the silence with, "Ummm . . . okay, Grandma, may I ask why someone would like to buy a square pear?"

She smiled. "Because it won't roll off the table. And I'm not just talking pears, dear, I am talking about square apples, oranges, the works. I'm talking about fruit that is normally round or roundish being square. Imagine it, no more fruit bowls to hold all that pesky round fruit. You could simply stack your fruit like blocks!" After she said this she made the motions of stacking blocks to give us a visual model.

"That's definitely interesting, Grandma, but how does it change the world for the better? That is what we should be focusing on here. We need an experiment that makes the world better. An invention that takes something that bothers us in the world and makes it better."

"Round fruit bothers me," she said in a very serious tone. "Just imagine it, Keith."

"I am imagining it, and I just don't know what to think. I don't really mind my fruit round. But if you really are interested in it, email the scientists at

Mr. Gonzalez's lab and they can talk more about it with you."

"Thanks, boss!" Grandma said, taking her seat again.

"I'm not the boss," I said. "I'm just, well, I don't know what I am exactly."

"You are in charge, son. That is what you are. And we will come up with something amazing to blow everyone away at your next science fair," Dad said.

"Yeah, Farts," Anthony said. "You can count on us."

That's what I'm concerned about, I thought.

So I was now running a company with no name and, as far as I could see, no ideas.

CHAPTER 7

I Have No Idea

Monday morning at six o'clock I sat at my desk in my room staring at my calendar. It was October 4. I flipped to November 15 and wrote "Mr. Gonzalez returns," and then turned to November 22 and wrote "Science Fair and *Helen Winifred Show*." I also realized that the fair was the week of Thanksgiving. I didn't know how thankful I'd be feeling, given the way things were going.

No one else was awake yet, so I went downstairs and just sat at the kitchen table for a while. It was nice to sit in complete quiet for a change. It had been a crazy weekend, between the interviews, seeing Mr. Gonzalez, the barf fest, and realizing our ideas were limited to fart experiments and square fruit. I was definitely in trouble. I had to think of something quick.

I poured a bowl of cereal and a glass of orange juice. Then I got the feeling that someone was watching me. You just know when someone is watching you. I turned around, and Emma was sitting at the table. "Good morning, Emma," I said, taking a bite. I felt a little bad because I realized I hadn't spent any time with Emma the whole weekend. I walked over and gave her a kiss on the forehead.

She immediately rattled one off the wooden kitchen chair. "Blueberry today, big brothu," she whispered and gave me two thumbs up.

Wow, I thought, *Mom was right.* Emma was getting a little carried away with the farting. She didn't seem to understand that even though I had fixed the smell of farts, it was still not something to be done around others. I decided it was time to have a big-brother-to-little-sister talk.

"Emma," I began, "you know that you can't keep making bubbles any time you like, right? It's not polite."

"Yeah, I know. I just think it's fun." She was smiling the cutest smile you've ever seen.

"Okay, but you know not to do it in places like school and stuff, right?"

"Why not? They smell so pretty. I eat a different

scent every day. Tomorrow I'm looking forward to tangaween." Still smiling.

"You mean tangerine." I wasn't sure what to say to her.

Just then Mom walked in. "Good morning, you guys," she said. "Keith, I see you have breakfast. Emma, darling, what would you like for breakfast?"

"I want candy, please," Emma said with a big smile on her face.

"Emma, you can't have candy," I reminded her.

"Well, that's what I want," she replied.

"What else do you like for breakfast?" I asked her.

"Besides candy?"

"Yes."

"*Welllll,* pretty much nothing."

I looked at Mom. She made a face as if to say, "I told you so." "Emma, I am making you pancakes, and you will have fifteen minutes to eat them."

"I don't like pancakes. I want candy— *hmmmmph!*" Emma said, crossing her arms. She seemed to think that crossing her arms would make everyone listen to her. What she failed to realize was that it just made Mom mad.

"I'd love to hang around and see how this

plays out, but I need to get to school," I said. "I'm going to be at the lab after school today, so I won't see you guys until late. Grandma is going to pick me up and take me after school."

"I want to go to the lab," Emma whined.

"You can't, Emma. You're too young. Maybe when you are older you can come in and see it, okay?"

"I want to go right now."

I gave her another kiss on the forehead and said, "When you're older. I love you. Now, please take it easy with all the farting today."

Emma looked up at me with her big eyes and tore another one off the seat. "Blueberry again. Enjoy, everybody," she said, laughing.

Mom rolled her eyes in disgust.

"Like I said, I have to get going." I grabbed my backpack and headed for the door.

"Keith," my mom called after me.

"Yeah?"

"Thanks again for Sweet Farts," she said sarcastically. "It's really changed my life for the better. I know you're very busy right now, but you are going to have to help me with your sister. She is getting out of control with this."

I thought it was odd that my mom was putting

this on me. She was the mom, after all. Shouldn't she be the one doing the raising of my sister?

"I'll try, Mom, but I'm pretty nuts right now, with Mr. Gonzalez coming back in six weeks, and the science fair, and *The Helen Winifred Show* on the twenty-second."

"Please tell me you are not going on *The Helen Winifred Show*. Please tell me your sister's gas has caused me to enter a dreamlike state and this is not my reality. I have been embarrassed enough with all this Sweet Farts hoopla already. I don't think I could take you going on my favorite show and talking about farts."

"I'm going to invent something new, Mom. Don't worry, it's going to be fine this time."

"Well, then what are you doing this year for the fair?" she asked.

"I have no idea. I have absolutely no idea," I admitted.

"Fantastic, that makes me feel much better," she said. "Just know that every mom in America watches that show." Then Mom stopped and the color drained from her face. She ran to her calendar. "Did you say November 22?"

"Yeah, why?"

"Because that is the Thanksgiving episode,

Keith! It's one of the biggest shows of the year. Wonderful—my son is going to be on Helen Winifred's show Thanksgiving week to talk about how he fixed farts." She was shaking the calendar around and holding it in front of her. "The other moms are never going to let me live this down, you know."

"Mom?" Emma interrupted.

"Yes, Emma?"

"You don't like the word *faawwt,* remembow?"

Mom looked defeated. I turned and grabbed my backpack and ran out the door.

CHAPTER 8
We ♥ Farts

I noticed a weird energy the minute I got on the school bus. Kids were looking at me and giggling and then looking away. I couldn't put my finger on it, but something was going on.

Scott got on and sat next to me. He had his jacket zipped all the way up to his neck. He never has his jacket zipped. Mr. Cherub is always telling him to zip up or he will get sick, but Scott is one of those kids who won't wear a coat even if it is freezing out. So the jacket, on and zipped, was suspicious.

"What's going on today, Scott?"

"Nothing. Just another Monday in paradise, my friend."

"I mean, why is everyone acting funny? And why is your jacket on and zipped all the way up?"

"My jacket is on because it is cold out and I am going to start listening to my teacher, Mr. Cherub."

"I don't believe that for a second. What's going on?" I looked around the bus again and everyone's eyes darted away from mine.

"It is just another day in paradise. I'm not sure what to tell you," he replied with a smile.

Something was up, but I couldn't figure out what. When we reached school, Scott and I got off the bus. We made our way into the building, down the hall, and finally into the classroom. That's when I realized what was up. Everyone in the class had on the same button, including Mr. Cherub. The button read "We Heart Farts," but instead of the word *heart* there was a picture of a heart. I turned to Scott, who had taken off his jacket to reveal his button.

"You're welcome," he said with a smile and headed off to his seat.

"Keith, good morning. I hope you had a nice weekend," Mr. Cherub began. "Your friends got together and got us all these buttons in order to support you as you make your final approach to the science fair."

"I don't understand. Isn't the entire class doing science-fair projects?" I asked.

"Of course, but yours is the only one that will be on *The Helen Winifred Show*. Yours is the only one that will represent our school worldwide. Yours is the one we are all counting on." I thought it was funny how Mr. Cherub was so against my science-fair idea last time and now he was so encouraging, even though he didn't know what it was.

Across the room, Scott pointed to his button and winked at me.

I felt a hand grab my shoulder from behind. "Good morning, Farts," Anthony greeted me.

"I said I don't want to be called Farts, Anthony."

"Too late, pal. Just have fun with it today, okay? Try not to be so uptight."

I turned and headed for my seat. Along the way I was called Farts by just about everyone in the class. Where had all these buttons come from?

Just then the morning announcements began. The principal's voice came over the PA system: "Good morning, Harborside Elementary! I wish to extend a special Harborside good morning to our science whiz Keith Emerson. Keith, we are all so proud of your accomplishments with inventing Sweet Farts last year, and we can't wait to see what you come up with for this year's science fair. We're proud of you, Farts—I mean, Keith. In other school news . . ."

His voice just sort of trailed off. I didn't hear anything else. I was lost in my own worries. As I looked around the room, it hit me. This year's fair was going to be terrible. Before I invented Sweet Farts no one expected anything from me. This year the expectations were off the charts. They thought I was a great scientist. What was I going to do? Then I heard the words no kid ever wants to hear in the morning announcements: "Keith Emerson, please come to the principal's office right away."

CHAPTER 9

No Pressure

I walked into the principal's office cautiously. The last time I was in Mr. Michaels' office he had ordered me to complete my Sweet Farts experiment, and I was pretty sure this meeting wasn't going to be good.

"Keith," he began, "have a seat." He leaned back in his chair. "Keith, I want to say how proud the whole school community is of you. By inventing Sweet Farts you have brought a great deal of attention to our little school. As you know, I am a huge Benjamin Franklin fan." He pointed to a picture of Benjamin Franklin on the wall behind me.

"Yes, sir, I remember you telling me that before."

"Well, as a fan of Mr. Franklin, I take very

seriously the fact that when you invented Sweet Farts you were able to successfully complete a scientific challenge the great Benjamin Franklin created. What you did was historic. Benjamin Franklin wrote in 1781 that if anyone could cure the smell of human gas, it would be the greatest scientific discovery of all time, and you, Keith, have met that challenge."

"I know, Mr. Michaels. We have talked about this countless times."

"I just want to make sure," he went on, "that you understand the importance of what you have done. You are on a path to greatness. If you play your cards right, you could be a truly great scientist."

"Thank you, sir, but I still don't get why you have me down here. I should probably get back to class."

"Keith, Mr. Gonzalez is one of the most respected scientific minds in the world. He sees something in you. I see something in you. I just want to make sure that you are not wasting your newfound independence playing sports and video games over at your new lab." He leaned forward, looking concerned.

"Well, I wouldn't say I have been wasting my

time. Just the other day we had a great meeting and we knocked around a few ideas." I left out the fact that they were all terrible.

"Good! I'm glad to hear you are on the ball. I would hate to see the science fair come along and you miss the opportunity to wow the world once again." When he said this I felt a rush of nervous energy run from the tip of my toes to the top of my head. I had never felt that kind of pressure. The scary truth was that there was a very good chance I would fail. For goodness' sake, I had no idea what I was going to do!

"I also wanted to tell you that I am allowing Scott and Anthony to help you and have the work they do count toward their projects. But that is entirely up to you. It is your company, after all. If you want their help, great. If not, they will be responsible for their own projects."

"I'll think about it, Mr. Michaels." I thought about their Silencer idea. "Right now we seem to be thinking of different ideas, but we will figure it out."

We shook hands and stood. I noticed that his tie read "We Heart Farts." "By the way," he said, "have you decided on a company name yet?"

I shook my head. "I'm still working on that, too, Mr. Michaels."

As I left his office, two very frightening thoughts went through my mind. Number one was that I really had no idea what I was going to do for the fair. Number two was that Scott and Anthony actually had an idea already. Those two knuckleheads were further along than I was! I noticed I was biting my nails as I walked down the hall toward class.

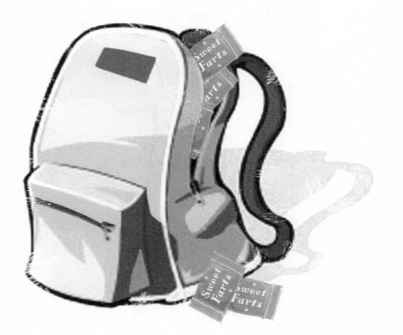

CHAPTER 10

Show and Smell

Later that night Grandma dropped me off at home. We had been working at the lab for several hours and it was after eight. Emma was already in bed. When I walked in, Mom and Dad were at the dinner table. They seemed pretty serious.

"What's going on, guys?" I asked.

"Well, son, your sister had show and tell today at school. Would you like to guess what she brought in to show all her little friends?" Dad asked.

"A teddy bear?" I asked hopefully.

"No," my mom interrupted. "She brought in a backpack jammed full of Sweet Farts packets. She talked for twenty minutes about how much she loves to pass gas. Her teacher said she actually passed gas several times during her presentation, for crying out loud! The teacher wants to have a parent-teacher conference with your dad and me first thing tomorrow morning!" Mom got up and walked into the kitchen to put her plate in the sink. She looked like she was about to cry.

I looked at my dad. He had his hand in front of his mouth like he was thinking really hard, but when I looked closer I could see that he was trying not to laugh. He wouldn't look at me. You know how it is when you are trying hard not to crack up. He knew if he looked at me he would lose it.

"Wow, Mom," I said in a loud voice so she could hear me in the kitchen. "Dad seems pretty upset about this, he won't even look at me." I sat down in the chair right across from him.

Mom walked back into the room and sat next to me. "Come on, Keith. You and I know that your dad is just trying to keep from laughing," she said as my dad finally burst into hysterics.

"I can't help it," Dad gasped. "I just keep getting the image in my head of Emma talking for twenty minutes in class about farts. It just strikes me as so funny. She called it 'show and smell.'" Tears were rolling down his cheeks. My mother and I did not crack even the slightest smile. Dad would stop for a second and then just lose control again.

"Of course," he managed to say, "this is no joking matter." He stood up and tried his best to be serious. "I—I can't help it," he said, wiping tears from his eyes as he left the room.

My mom made a face. "Your father will be back once he gets control of himself. We need a plan with her, Keith. It's not just the gas passing with her lately. She isn't eating. You were tough to feed when you were her age, but she is getting scary with it. I am taking her to the doctor tomorrow after school because she isn't gaining weight like she should."

"Aren't kids supposed to stay thin to be healthy?" I asked.

"Yes, but your sister is getting to the point where she doesn't want anything but candy and chips. She won't eat any sort of meat, vegetable, or fruit. I haven't even been able to get her to eat pizza lately."

"What do you mean? She seriously won't eat anything healthy?" I asked, concerned. "What has she been eating?

"I can't remember the last time she ate anything that wasn't a pretzel or a lollipop."

"Seriously?"

"Yes, I don't want to alarm you, Keith, but

this is a real problem. I weighed her the other day, and she had actually lost weight this month. That is not a good thing for a growing girl."

I couldn't help but think that if my parents tried a little harder they would be able to get Emma to eat something healthy.

"I'll get up early tomorrow morning and make her a special breakfast," I said. "I'll get that kid to eat. You'll see."

CHAPTER 11

Anthony Goes Rogue

The next day at school went pretty smoothly. Thank goodness there were no meetings with the principal and no surprises like yesterday, although I was called Farts more times than I could count. I kept waiting for someone to call me Keith or even S.B.D. for old times' sake, but it never happened. Anthony and Scott had successfully erased my name from existence and renamed me Farts.

Grandma picked me up at school along with Anthony and Scott, and we were all at the lab by three thirty. Grandma went straight to her room to get to work. "Fruit isn't going to get square all on its own, boys," she said as she walked down the hall.

I got to work right away. "Okay, guys," I said as we sat at the table having a snack. "It is no secret that I have no ideas for the science fair. I was thinking about it today, and I think part of the problem is that we have no company name yet. We have all this cool stuff, and Sweet Farts is available everywhere, but we don't have a name. Mr. Gonzalez has his company, Gonzalez World Wide. We need a name already."

"Yeah," Scott added. "We do need a name. We could also use a website. That way we can post what we are working on so kids at school stop asking me. I'm getting tired of explaining the Silencer all day long."

"Okay, any ideas?" I asked.

"I have it," Anthony announced: "The Fart Factory!" He clapped his hands once and got up out of his seat. "Boom! That was easy! Now let's get back to work. You're welcome, Farts."

"No, not the Fart Factory," I said. "I want to break away from the whole fart image. It's getting to be a little too much. I was S.B.D. last year, and now I'm Farts, thank you very much, and I need the company name to be something more classy."

"You invented something that makes farts smell good," Scott added. "How classy do you expect to get?"

"I don't know. I just think if we put our minds to it . . ." At that moment I got a whiff of something I haven't smelled in a very long time. At first I started to gag a little, but then I recovered and held it back. It didn't compute in my brain for a split second, and then it hit me. For the first time in months I smelled a fart! Not a new and improved Sweet Farts fart, I smelled an old-fashioned gross-you-out job. It hit Scott an instant later.

"*Ooohhhh, no!*" he shouted. "What's going on?" He was holding his nose as he jumped out of his seat and ran toward the back door. He ran out the door and didn't come back.

Anthony just stood in front of me and put a hand on my shoulder. "Sorry, dude!" he said proudly. "I'm over your little invention. I'm bringing farting back to the old days."

"What are you talking about?" I said, trying to wave it out of the air. "That was so gross I can't even get over it."

"I'm saying to you here and now, I am off the Sweet Farts. They just aren't me. I'm an organic kind of guy. It just seemed fake and artificial to me. From now on I will be rippin' it old-school."

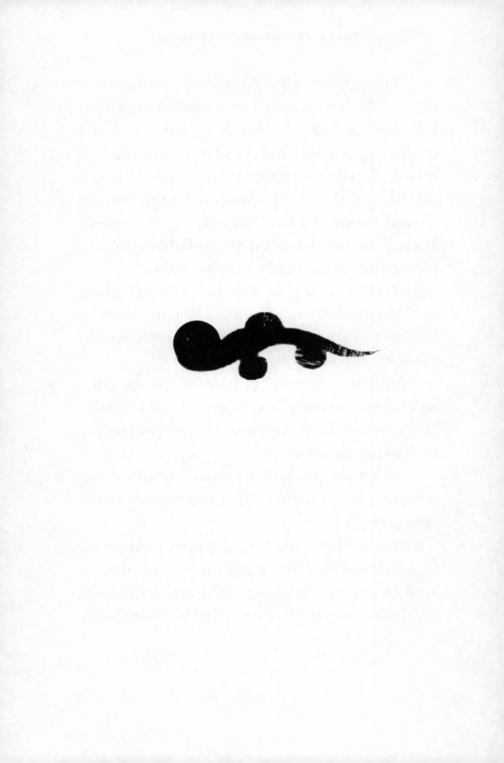

CHAPTER 12

The Family Business

That night Grandma dropped me off at around eight. Emma was in bed. Mom and Dad were at the table. It was like the night before all over again.

"I'm afraid to ask," I said.

"How about starting with 'I'm sorry,'" Mom said.

"Why should I be sorry?" I asked.

"If I recall, you said last night that you were going to wake up and make Emma a great big breakfast. You said not to worry."

"Oh my gosh! I completely forgot. I am so sorry, Mom. I wanted to, and then I was just so caught up in my own stuff that I completely forgot." I slapped my forehead in frustration.

"It's okay," she said. "It wouldn't have helped anyway. She ate nothing today. The doctor told me to stop giving in to her and letting her have whatever she wants. She said that when Emma was ready to eat good food, she would eat. So today your sister ate nothing at all from the time she woke up to the time she went to bed." Mom looked like she was going to cry. Dad wasn't laughing tonight.

"Oh yeah, and then there's the teacher's conference today," my dad said. "I know I joke around a lot, but we really have to watch it with your sister. She is really going over the edge with this Sweet Farts stuff. The teacher said she told the class farts are her family business. Which I guess is correct in a way, but she needs to ease up."

My mom added, "I'm relieved to hear your father say that because I am going to need help from both of you with Emma."

"I'm sorry I've been so crazy, Mom. I promise to try and help more with Emma. I am just completely freaking about my project. The pressure this time around is too much, and the guys aren't helping out."

"I noticed," Mom said. "I read the articles from the interviews you did. I'm so sorry they are calling you Farts now."

"Yeah, tell me about it. I thought after being called S.B.D. any change would be nice, but Farts is not what I was hoping for." Then something happened that hadn't happened between me and Mom in a while: We both started laughing. We weren't just laughing about my nickname. We were laughing at all the crazy stuff that had been going on lately. The laughter helped melt away some of the stress, and it felt good to see Mom relax for a change.

Then I smelled it. It was familiar and foreign at the same time. Dad got up. "I think I will be heading off to bed," he said. "It's getting late, and I bid you both a good evening." He bowed and began to back out of the room.

"Honey, you can't be serious," Mom said as she covered her mouth and nose.

"Sweetie, I am doing this for Emma. She has to be reminded of how horrible farts are. Until further notice, I am off Sweet Farts," he announced and ran out of the room.

I looked at Mom in disbelief. "Can you believe this? To make matters worse, Anthony stopped taking Sweet Farts too. Now the two people who caused me to want to invent Sweet Farts in the first place are refusing to take it. What is happening?"

"I don't know, but if your father isn't going to take Sweet Farts, I might just grind them up in his breakfast every morning. I have enough to worry about with Emma. I am not going back to the smelly old days with your father before Sweet Farts."

"So you admit it," I said smiling.

"Admit what?"

"Admit that Sweet Farts made your life better."

"I am proud that you were smart enough to think of such an amazing invention. Just do me a favor: This time, invent something the other moms won't laugh about behind my back, okay?"

"I'll try, Mom, but I can't promise anything."

CHAPTER 13

What Happens When You Don't Eat?

The rest of the week went by pretty much the same. Anthony and Dad continued to punish the rest of us with reminders of why I had invented Sweet Farts in the first place, Grandma stayed locked up in her lab room working away on making fruit square, and Emma didn't eat. She had gone almost a whole day without so much as a glass of water when Mom finally gave in and let her eat anything she wanted. Emma chose fruit snacks. Mom seemed relieved that Emma's choice at least had the word *fruit* in it. The fact that it was basically sugar and food coloring was beside the point—Emma had eaten something!

Unfortunately it was the only thing she would now eat.

So at breakfast Emma had one small bag of fruit snacks, at lunch Emma had one small bag of fruit snacks, and at dinner Emma had one small bag of fruit snacks. That was it—nothing more, nothing less. Emma was really worrying me.

I sat at my computer Saturday night. The stress of Emma was really getting to me. Also, when I worry about too many things my mind starts to go all over the place. I decided to search on the computer to find some answer to Emma's situation. I typed into the search box "What happens when you don't eat?"

I clicked on the first site that came up. The response to my question was "You die."

I read through a few more sites and they said the same thing only in nicer terms. Emma definitely had to eat, and I wasn't sure how to help. I decided I would get up in the morning for real this time and see if I could get her to eat.

Then I started thinking about ideas for my science-fair project. I typed: "The Problem."

I sat there for a long time thinking about what problem I wanted to solve. The only problem I could think of was the fact that I did not have a problem I wanted to solve. Maybe I should just join Grandma and try to think of a way to grow square pears. Or I could help Anthony and Scott try to make farts silent—although I didn't think I could handle another fart experiment. Dad wouldn't be any help—as far as I knew, Dad hadn't been in the lab since the day of the barf fest. He was probably afraid to come back.

I finally decided to go to bed and start fresh the next day. I saved my work on the computer. It read simply, "The Problem: I have no ideas."

CHAPTER 14

Welcome to the Fart Palace

Sunday morning I woke up late. I opened my eyes, and the clock read eleven fifteen. I was amazed that I'd slept that long, because I almost never sleep that late. I felt rested for the first time in a long time. Then my relaxed feeling melted away as I realized I had slept through breakfast.

I jumped out of bed and ran downstairs in my pajamas. Dad was asleep on the couch, Mom was on her computer researching how to get kids to eat, and Emma was watching a show. I shut off Emma's show with the remote.

"Hey! What's the big idea, brothow?" Emma demanded.

"It's *brother* with an *er* at the end, not *brothow* with an *ow* at the end. And you are coming in the kitchen with me to cook, little lady."

"I can cook with you?" she asked, excited.

"Yes, you can. We are going to make some delicious food together. What do you say?"

Mom smiled at me, and I think she had a little bit of a "happy cry," as she likes to call them. It made me feel good to be helping out and not worrying about my own problems.

"What are we making?" Emma asked.

"We are going to make my famous vegetable stir-fry," I said. Vegetable stir-fry was the only thing I knew how to cook. When I was in third grade I thought I wanted to be a chef, so I went on the computer and looked up how to make my favorite food at the time, which was vegetable stir fry. My mom helped me make it, and I've been making it ever since. I did lose my passion for being a chef once I had to clean up all the cutting boards and pans. But I had learned how to make one thing—and vegetable stir-fry was about to become Emma's new favorite, too. I could feel it. I was about to save the day.

Emma helped me take all the vegetables out of the fridge. She helped me wash them, and after I

had cut them she put them all in a dish. After I'd cut each vegetable I tried to get her to taste it, but she wouldn't. We cut carrots, broccoli, tomatoes, string beans, and even the little baby corns. Emma ate nothing.

I had her help me mix together all my secret ingredients for the sauce. In a bowl she mixed soy sauce, wasabi, teriyaki, brown sugar, garlic, onion, and chicken stock. Then she helped me make brown rice. She measured it out in a measuring cup and poured it into the water for me. I was sure that if she ate anything at all it would be the brown rice with a little of my famous sauce.

When we were done, the kitchen was an absolute mess. It was twelve thirty, and I was exhausted. I had Emma spoon some stir-fry onto four different plates. She walked the plates to the table, and then we poured lemonade into four glasses. She was having a ball.

When everything was ready I told her we could pretend it was a fancy restaurant and get dressed up. The food was hot, and I figured this would be a great way to let it cool off and keep her excited about eating.

"Can I wear my pink dress with the stripes?" she asked. "The one Grandma got me?"

"You sure can," I said. "Just hurry up, because we don't want it to get cold."

"And my fancy black shoes?" she added as she ran toward her room.

"Sure," I said.

She disappeared into her room like a bolt. I ran up to my room and quickly put on my one and only suit. As I put the tie around my neck and straightened it in the mirror I was feeling pretty proud of myself. Why hadn't my parents thought of this? Maybe I was a great mind after all. I mean, they had been dealing with this problem for a while. They had talked to the teacher and the doctor, and now I was about to solve the Emma eating problem on my first try.

I ran back downstairs and sat down at the dinner table. Emma came racing in a second later.

"You look beautiful, Emma. This food sure smells delicious. I can't wait to eat it. Why don't you go get Mom and Dad in here," I told her.

She gave me two thumbs up and ran out of the room smiling. Just a few more minutes and I would be a hero. I could barely take the excitement.

Mom and Dad walked in together. "Welcome to our restauwant," Emma said proudly.

"Wow," Dad said. "What's this all about?" He winked at me as he took his seat. Mom looked really happy too. She didn't even seem to mind that Emma didn't pronounce the second R in *restaurant*. It was a pretty awesome feeling. They were pretty lucky to have a kid like me around.

"What is the name of your lovely restaurant, Emma dear?" Mom inquired.

"I don't know," she said, looking at me. "What is our restauwant called?"

"Anything you like, Emma," I said in my sweetest voice.

She tapped her finger on the side of her head for a moment, as if she was thinking real hard, and said, "I got it!"

"What?" Mom asked, glowing.

"My restauwant is called Emma's Fart Palace," she said and fell out of her seat laughing.

Dad started to laugh and then caught himself. "Emma, farts are not funny," he began. "Do you want Daddy to drop one and show you what I mean?" he said seriously.

"No!" I cried. "For the love of all that's sensible, are you serious right now, Dad? Emma, if you want to call it the Fart Palace, then go right ahead. I for one can't wait to eat." I picked up my fork and took a bite. "This is wonderful, Emma," I said as I stared at my parents, waiting for them to follow my lead.

Mom followed my lead and took a bite. "Oh, honey, you have got to try this."

Dad finally got with the program and had a bite, too. "Wow, this is great, Emma!"

"Why don't you have a bite, Emma?" I asked.

"*Naaah*," she said. "I don't like food, remembow?"

"You can't have a restaurant and not eat, though," I said cleverly.

Just then Emma noticed that she had a fairly large stain on her beautiful pink dress with the stripes. It looked like it was soy sauce.

"Oh, no!" she shouted. "My dress is ruined."

"It's okay," my mom said. "I can fix your dress, Emma. Don't worry."

Emma started crying like crazy. She went to get up out of her seat and accidentally knocked her plate off the table and onto her fancy black shoes. At that point her crying turned into hysterics.

"Get it off!" she shouted.

Mom jumped up and tried to calm Emma down. Dad looked like he was in complete shock. I couldn't believe this was happening. I tried telling Emma it was all right, but she was so upset that there was no sense in talking to her.

As Mom was trying to wipe the vegetable stir-fry off Emma's shoes, Emma started to run, and when she started to run, she slipped. When she slipped, she fell face-first into a giant pile of vegetable stir-fry. When she raised her face it was covered in brown sauce. Rice and vegetables dangled from her hair, and she screamed, "I hate food!" and ran for her room.

CHAPTER 15

Grandma's Room

That week came and went in the blink of an eye. Emma continued to eat candy and chips, Mom continued to worry, and Dad—well, I'm not exactly sure what Dad did, but I sure smelled him a few times. Me, I still hadn't moved beyond the problem stage of my project. I thought I had a few good ideas as the week went on, but nothing led to a clear plan for a project that I wanted to do for the fair. I was now down to five weeks until Mr. Gonzalez came back from Africa. The science fair was in six weeks.

I was at the lab hitting baseballs off the pitching machine in the back. It was pretty cold out, but I didn't care. The crack of the ball and the swinging of the bat were helping me think.

After about an hour my hands started to get cold, and I went inside. Anthony and Scott were busy in their room, working away. They had a few scientists from Mr. Gonzalez's lab with them. I decided to go down to Grandma's room for a while. When I walked into the room, my jaw dropped. I couldn't believe how many fruit trees she had crammed in there. Five or six scientists were busy poking and prodding the different trees. A woman was injecting a blue liquid into the base of a pear tree. Another scientist was spraying the tree's leaves with a bottle full of some kind of mist. Grandma was nowhere to be found.

"Excuse me," I said to the woman with the needle. "Have you seen my grandmother?"

The woman pointed up at the pear tree, which was about seventeen feet tall. I looked up to see Grandma at the top. She was wearing goggles and spraying that same mist on the pears hanging from the high branches.

"Hey, Bubble Gum!" she said, looking down at me. My grandmother has a habit of calling me random words as nicknames. She has called me Rock Star, Bean Pole, Jumping Jack, and my personal favorite, Mince Meat. Don't ask me why she does it or where they come from. It's just one of those things that make Grandma, Grandma.

She scurried down the tree in a flash. "What's the story, Morning Glory?" she asked.

"I just thought I'd come by and talk to you for a while. Are you free?"

"For you, I am always free. You know that." She handed her spray bottle to a scientist who was walking by. "Can you climb up there and keep working for me, please?"

"Sure, Grandma," he said. I was kind of surprised that even the scientists were calling her Grandma. Then again, it's hard to think of anyone calling her anything but Grandma, because she is such a grandma.

Grandma walked out of the room with her goggles still on, and I followed her. Anthony and Scott were on the court playing basketball with a few scientists. "Let's go somewhere quiet that we can talk," Grandma said.

"Follow me," I said. "I know the perfect place." We walked into my lab room.

Grandma's face sank when she saw the empty room. "Oh, sweetie, you really don't have anything going on in here, do you?"

"No," I said. "Why? Did you think I was kidding?"

"I thought you had to be working on something by now. I figured that you just weren't ready to talk about it. Okay, here's what we will do. I'll have the people in my room move everything in here tonight, and you will continue my great pear experiment."

"No, Grandma. I'm not looking for you to save me. I just wanted to spend some time with you."

"Oh, you sweet, sweet thing. I appreciate that, but Keith, darling, the fair is in less than five weeks. What are you planning on doing?" She looked as concerned as I felt.

"I'm not sure. I keep getting stuck. I'm so worried about doing well that I can't think at all."

"Like I said, I'll have them move the trees in here in the middle of the night. You will be the square pear man if it's the last thing I do. We aren't quite there yet, but we did grow an orange that was shaped like a banana! That's something, right?"

"I guess. It's just . . . I just don't know what to do."

"Just relax," she said. "Try not to think too much about it. What did you do last time?"

"Well, last time I was stuck, too. I had no idea what experiment to work on for the fair, and Mr. Cherub told me to think of something that bothers me in the world and change it for the better."

"So what is bothering you now?"

"That's the problem. I'm not sure."

"Just trust yourself and it will come to you. Now excuse me while I go change the fruit world forever. If you decide you want the square pear idea just say the word and it's yours."

CHAPTER 16
The Meeting

Before I knew it, another week had zipped by. It was already October 23. Grandma was plugging along on her idea, and Anthony and Scott seemed pretty busy with their project. We hadn't really spent a lot of time together, though. So I called a meeting.

"Okay, everyone, let's talk a little about what we have been doing and where we are with our projects. The science fair is four weeks away and Mr. Gonzalez comes back in three weeks. It is officially crunch time."

"Me and Anthony have parted ways," Scott said. "I can't stand the smell in there anymore. I've decided to give up on the Silencer because it is just a little too weird trying to invent something that silences farts. The scientists started talking to us about what might be involved, and I decided I don't want to spend the next month smelling farts. How did you handle that last time?"

"I have no idea," I said. "I was desperate, I guess. So what are you going to do for the fair?"

"I'm still thinking about it."

"Anthony, please tell me you have something!"

"As a matter of fact, I think I do, Prut," he said, smiling.

"What did you call me?" I asked.

Scott was smiling too.

"I called you Prut."

"What does that mean?"

"If you were Danish you would know," he teased.

"Well, I'm not Danish. It's not enough to call me names in English anymore? Now you're doing it in other languages? Thanks a lot."

Scott interrupted: "It means *fart* in Danish. Anthony and I found this amazing website that translates any word into every language you can think of. *Prut* means *fart* in Danish," he said again, looking proud of himself.

"I heard you the first time, Scott. I'm happy to hear you guys are making good use of your time here at the lab. Mr. Gonzalez would be very proud.

"Relax, Winderigheid," Anthony said, smiling. "That means *fart* in Dutch, in case you were wondering."

"I wasn't," I said in a frustrated tone. "Are you going to tell me your idea or not?"

Anthony began. "It is an unknown fact at Harborside Elementary that I am a bit of a math whiz. Ever since I was real little, I could remember all kinds of crazy facts about baseball players, like batting averages and stuff."

"So?" I said.

"So I realized that I'm pretty good at finding patterns in players' statistics. I sometimes can predict when a guy is going to get a hit or strike out based on his previous at bats."

"So?"

"So I think I can take my gift of understanding patterns and use it to predict the lottery numbers. I am going to become a millionaire, Farts. I'm tired of riding your coattails."

"Anthony, no offense, but you cannot predict the lottery numbers just because you are good at predicting baseball. And what about the Silencer?"

"The Silencer grew tiresome. And as far as I can tell, I have a hypothesis and you two have nothing but a nose full of this"—and Anthony let one go.

Scott didn't say a word—he ran for the back door again. I shook my head. I couldn't figure Anthony out. He didn't care what anyone thought. He never seemed to get embarrassed.

"Excuse me while I go and try to make my fortune," Anthony said, and he walked down the hall toward his room.

"We still need a name for the company!" I yelled.

CHAPTER 17

Whatevoh

The whole next week the only thing I did was work on my swing. I had come to the realization that the fair was going to be a complete failure. Mr. Gonzalez would come back from Africa and all I would have to show him would be Grandma's fruit trees and Anthony's numbers. He would kick me out of the lab and that would be the end of it all. Halloween came and went, and I didn't even trick-or-treat. I was too worried about the fair.

I woke up on the morning of November 1 knowing two things: First, I was going to lose the lab. That was a certainty. Second, I was about to be humiliated in front of the school, my family, and the whole world on *The Helen Winifred Show*. I started to get a surge of anxiety again. When

I get worried like that my mind just locks in on my worries and I can't get free. No matter how hard I tried to think of other things, my mind just wouldn't let up.

I pictured myself at the science fair: All the other kids would have their experiments finished. All the parents and teachers would be walking from room to room, checking out the projects. I could see myself in front of an empty desk. When people walked by and asked me where my project was, I would just shrug.

Then an idea hit me.

I could say that my experiment involved some element of invisibility and that in the process of experimenting, the project had become invisible. The only problem was that if it were invisible, you would still be able to touch it. Invisibility was a crazy idea.

"Keith!" I heard Mom shout from downstairs. "Your bus is going to be here in a few minutes." I bolted out of bed and ran for the bathroom. Along the way I looked out the window and saw that it was snowing for the first time that year. I ran back to my room to put a thermal undershirt on. Coming out of my room with the thermal still half over my head, I almost ran straight into Emma.

"Wow! Watch out, Emma," I said as I sidestepped her. She just kept on running and went into my room.

I turned around and followed her.

"Hey, what's going on, Emma?" She was lying in my bed with the covers pulled up over her head.

"I'm not going to school today," she wailed. "I'm not going to school today or any other day." I could tell that she was crying because her voice had that cracking sound it makes when you can't get your words out.

"Emma, come on. Of course you're going to school today. Why don't you tell me what is going on."

"Mommy just told me that if I don't eat breakfast she won't let me play with any of my toys anymore."

"Emma, Mommy is just worried about you. She doesn't want to see you get sick. If you don't eat, you won't grow, and your body won't be healthy. Nobody wants that to happen."

"It's just that everything I eat tastes gross except for candy and chips. I can eat healthy when I'm oldow. For now I want to eat candy and chips."

"Keith!" Mom shouted again. "You're going to miss the bus, and I am not driving you today. The roads are horrible. You had better hurry up!"

I grabbed my backpack. "I'm sorry, Emma. I

have to go. Maybe we can talk after school today."

"Whatevoh," she said sadly. "You won't be home for a long time, and I'll already be in bed." She was crying even harder.

"I'll try to get home early, Emma. I promise," I said as I ran out the door and headed for the bus.

CHAPTER 18

Go Gooz

I made the bus right before my bus driver, Mrs. Grimp, closed the door and left me there.

"I was about to leave without you, Farts!" she said matter-of-factly. I didn't feel it was entirely appropriate for the bus driver to be calling me Farts, but then again, everyone seemed to be calling me Farts these days.

"You should leave more time on snowy days. I thought you were supposed to be some sort of genius or something. Until you invent a way to get yourself to school on time, I expect you to be at this stop and ready when I pull up. Now go sit down."

"Good morning to you, too, Mrs. Grimp," I said. I walked back to my seat next to Scott. He gets on the bus at his aunt's house on days his mom works. On those days he is on the bus before me.

The bus pulled away before I was actually sitting, and I half fell into the seat.

Before I could say a word Scott handed me a T-shirt and said, "Put this on."

"What is it?"

"There's this new kid in third grade—he moved here about a week ago. He's going to run in a marathon to raise money for some charity thing his parents are involved in. The marathon is this weekend, so we are all wearing these shirts to support him. The company paid for shirts for the whole school. You're a pretty generous guy," he said with a grin.

"Next time, how about asking first?" I said. "How come I never heard of this kid? A third grader running a marathon? Isn't that like twenty-six miles or something?"

"Twenty-six point two miles, to be exact. Now put the shirt on."

I held up the shirt. It read, "Go Gooz."

"The kid's name is Gooz? What kind of name is Gooz, anyway?" I asked.

"I don't know. His last name is Gooz. I didn't name him," Scott said, looking out the window at the snow.

"Why did we pay for these? How come the

school didn't pay for them, or the kid's family?"

"Because I told the principal we would take care of it. Don't worry about it. It's a good thing for the company. We can write it off on your taxes this year as a charitable contribution."

"What do you know about taxes?" I asked.

"I just know some stuff. Your company, whatever it's called, is going to need write-offs. I think what you're trying to say is 'Thank you.'"

"I am definitely not trying to say 'Thank you.' Scott, if you are messing with me I am going to be super mad." I wanted to believe Scott, but there was a part of me that sensed something was up, even though the shirt didn't say anything about me. It was all about this Gooz kid, and it did seem like a good cause, even though I wished we hadn't paid for the shirts.

I took my jacket off and put the shirt on over my thermal. Then I put my jacket back on.

"That a boy," Scott said. "Good for you. It will do you good to do something nice for someone else for a change. I don't know if you've noticed, but you've become pretty focused on yourself lately. All you do is stress about this science fair, and you never talk about anything else or have any fun. What kid doesn't go trick-or-treating for Halloween? Also, do you know you haven't once come in to see what Anthony and I are working on?"

"Who knows, maybe you're right. I *have* been stressed-out lately. What are you working on, anyway? I know Anthony is working on his lottery thing."

"I'm not saying what I'm working on, but I think you'll be impressed with my project."

The bus came to a stop and we both got off. We walked in the building and down the hall to our class. As I entered I noticed that other kids were wearing the Go Gooz shirt as well. I hung my jacket on the hook in my cubby and sat down at my desk. The announcements hadn't been made yet, so kids were still busy sharpening pencils and talking. Anthony sat down at his desk in front of me.

"Hey, Keith," he said, "sorry we didn't tell you about the Goozer until this morning. It's just that you've been so focused on the fair we didn't want to bother you." I almost fell out of my chair. Had Anthony just called me Keith and said 'sorry' in the same sentence?

"Thanks, Anthony. That means a lot to me. I haven't heard of this Gooz kid, but I think it's pretty cool that you guys did this. You even got

Mr. Cherub a Go Gooz tie, I see."

"Yeah," he said, smiling. "Isn't it awesome? Gooz is going to love this."

The bell rang and the daily announcements started.

I began my morning work. I felt relaxed for the first time in a while. I was still thinking about Emma, though. I felt bad that I hadn't been around for her that much lately. I decided to skip the lab and go straight home.

Just then I got a whiff.

"Come on, Anthony," I said. I held my nose and looked around the room for support.

"Keith, please wait until the announcements are completed to talk," Mr. Cherub said. The class was giving me the look, as if they thought I had done it.

"It wasn't me," I announced to the class. "I invented Sweet Farts, remember? It was Anthony."

"Keith, remember the other day when you told me you were going rogue and that you were off the Sweet Farts?" Anthony blurted out.

"No," I insisted. "That was you."

"Keith, we all know you invented Sweet Farts because your farts are so awful. Just own it already. You have horrible gas. It's okay to admit that now."

He turned around in his chair to look at me. He was smiling from ear to ear.

It was like old times. I froze up. I felt the nervous energy running wild in my body, and I couldn't get out any words. Mr. Cherub finally said, "Boys, you have been getting along pretty well this year. Let's not ruin things now on Gooz's big day." The class started to get the giggles. The way people were looking at me, I couldn't tell if they thought I had just farted or if something else was going on. Too many people were looking at me. Something was going on.

That was all that was said between Anthony and me. I was pretty much over the whole thing anyway. If the class still thought I was the one who was farting all this time, so be it.

"Line up for gym, please," Mr. Cherub said. *Thank goodness,* I thought. Maybe I could release a little frustration running around in the gym. If I was lucky it would be dodgeball day and I could unload on Anthony.

I made sure I was at the end of the line to avoid being near Anthony. Mr. Elliott, the gym teacher, greeted us at the entrance to the gym. Mr. Elliott's thing was that he said *hi* to every kid as he or she walked through the door.

"Hi, Mary," he said. "Hi, Jennifer. Good morning, Paul"—and then it happened. I was right behind Paul, and as I walked by Mr. Elliott, who was wearing a Go Gooz tank top, he said quite clearly, "I'm rooting for you, Gooz," and gave me a hard gym-teacher slap on the back. Then he ran off and blew his whistle to get everyone's attention.

"Today we are going to be taking a nutrition test, so"—he held up a box of pencils and a handful of fill-in-the-blank sheets—"you will have to be quiet today in the gym while you take the test. My apologies."

I felt a hot boil begin to brew inside me. Kids were looking at me now and giggling to themselves. Why had Mr. Elliott just called me Gooz?

Everyone sat on the floor, and Mr. Elliott began to pass out the tests and pencils. I tried to make eye contact with Anthony or Scott, but neither one of them would look in my direction. Mr. Eliott finally reached me.

"Mr. Elliott," I whispered as I took my test.

"Yes, Keith?" he whispered back.

"Why did you call me Gooz as I walked into the gym just now?"

He smiled and said, "When Anthony and Scott gave me my tank top yesterday they said it means *farts* in a language called Farsi. Farts is your new nickname, isn't it?"

"Farsi?" I asked.

"Yes, I think people speak it in Pakistan." He pointed to my shirt and smiled. "I can't wait to see what your next invention is," he said seriously. Then he turned back to the class and chanted, "Go, Gooz!"

The class immediately chanted back, "Go, Gooz! Go, Gooz!" through the snickering that was breaking out all over the room.

Something blew inside me, like when you see those buildings on TV when they are being demolished. One minute they are there and the next they are exploding into dust. I blew like never before. I stood up and ran directly at Anthony and tried to dive on top of him. At the last minute, he moved quickly to his left, and I went flying into the rack of basketballs in front of him.

CHAPTER 19
The Talk

After a quick visit to the nurse's office to get ice for the lump on my head, I made my way down to the principal's office. Mr. Michaels was standing in the doorway and waved me into his office when he saw me coming.

"Have a seat, Keith," he said. "What exactly is going on with you, young man? Mr. Elliott said you attacked your friend Anthony in gym class."

"I am really stressed about the fair and then these guys go and pull this Go Gooz thing on me. I mean, *you're* even wearing a Go Gooz tie, Mr. Michaels. How am I supposed to handle this?"

"Keith, your friends are just having a little fun at your expense, but their hearts are in the right place. Plus, this has been great for school morale.

The T-shirts your company has donated have gone a long way toward getting everyone excited about the science fair. I'm thinking of giving Anthony and Scott school-spirit awards for supporting you the way they're doing."

"Supporting me? Those two have been torturing me for weeks and you are going to reward them? That's perfect. You know what? Go ahead, you might as well. That makes complete sense." *Maybe we should build a statue of the two of them pointing at me and laughing,* I thought.

"Keith, try to relax. You are only a few weeks away from sharing your next great invention with the world. Try to enjoy it. Whether you see it or not, your friends are there for you. Sometimes we don't realize how important friends are to us, even if they do make us crazy."

"No," I said, standing up, "I know exactly how I feel about my friends. I would be better off without them."

"I disagree. I think your friends are pushing you to be your best and you don't like the feeling."

"I don't know that I would call what they are doing encouraging."

"All I'm saying is, you have to let people be

themselves and enjoy your experience. If you do, maybe they won't mess with you the way they are. Now since *you* are the only one hurt by your outburst in gym class, I will let you off with a warning, but you had better keep your frustrations in check, Goozer," he said, playing with his tie.

I thanked Mr. M., although I was unsure why, and walked back to class. Before I walked in I took off my Go Gooz shirt and threw it in the garbage.

CHAPTER 20

Corn

I took the bus straight home after school. I didn't talk to Anthony or Scott for the rest of the day. I must have been called Gooz or Goozer a hundred times. The bus was no different. As I got off, Mrs. Grimp said, "Remember, tomorrow you're going to be on time. Right, Gooz?" I just shot her a look as I climbed down the steps.

I walked along the snow-covered street back to my house, feeling pretty crummy. It was bad enough that the fair was coming faster than lightning, but it was worse the way everyone was treating me.

I opened the front door and ran for my room. I felt the tears coming as I got to my door. I fell onto my beanbag chair facedown and started crying like crazy. There I was, ten years old and behaving like my kid sister had that morning. I was completely falling apart. Somehow I needed to figure out a way to get it together. At this pace I wouldn't even make it to the fair. I'd be hiding in my closet by the end of the week.

"What's going on, pal?" I heard my dad say.

"Yeah, honey, are you okay?" Mom added.

"Oh, I'm just great," I said through my tears. "I'm pretty much the laughingstock of my whole school, and after the fair I'm going to be the laughingstock of the whole world!" I couldn't believe how hard I was crying. It was like I was three again or something.

My parents both sat down on my floor next to me. "It's going to be okay, Keith," my mom said softly. "You'll figure out a way through it. You always do."

"Yeah, buddy," my dad added. "Things seemed pretty bad a few weeks before the last fair, too, and you pulled it off."

From under the blankets on my bed I heard, "Yeah, big brothow, you will figure something out." It was Emma. I sat up and wiped the tears from my eyes.

"Why are you in my bed?" I asked.

"I've been here all day," Emma said, pushing the covers off her head. "I had a bellyache this morning and Mommy let me stay home. I wanted to wait for you."

"You let her stay home all day?" I asked my mom.

"Yes, I'm worried about her. She seems weak and she wasn't feeling well. I don't know what else to do."

"Mom, you can't let her stay home from school and eat candy and chips. Emma, did you eat anything today besides candy or chips?" I asked.

"Yes," she said proudly.

"Really? What was it?" I said, full of excitement and wiping the final tears from my eyes.

"I had corn," she said.

"Good, Emma. Corn is really good for you."

"Keith," my mom interrupted. "It was candy corn."

CHAPTER 21

The Deal

Mom and Dad left my room and went to the kitchen to make a dinner that Emma definitely would not eat. I stayed in my room and tried to work on my computer. Emma was on the floor playing with her Hair Style Suzie doll. She was talking to herself as she played. I was amazed at how incredibly cute she sounded.

"Your hair is a mess, Suzie. It's a good thing you came in for your aportmin." She meant to say "appointment." She was pretending to cut the doll's hair with her plastic toy scissors.

I looked at my computer screen. I couldn't believe that I was still on the "Problem" portion of the scientific method. The word *problem* glared back at me as if taunting me. As if to say, "I dare you to think of a problem. You're no scientist. You got lucky last time."

"Emma," I said, "what would you do for the science fair if you were me?"

"That's easy," she said without hesitating. "I would invent something that makes chicken taste like candy canes."

That was it! My little sister had just solved my problem. I'd been driving myself nuts trying to find the thing in the world that bothered me most and it was right there in front of me all along. The thing that bothered me most right then was the fact that my sister wouldn't eat anything.

"You're a genius, Emma!"

"I know," she said as if it were the most obvious thing in the world.

The idea came out of nowhere. One minute I had no clue what my project would be and then, in an instant, it was there as clear as day. I started typing out the rest of the scientific method.

Problem/Question: Can I invent something that makes food taste and smell like another type of food? For example, can I make chicken taste like candy canes?

Then I clicked onto the Internet and typed in:

"Healthy foods kids hate to eat?"

I read a bunch of information about how liver is a healthy food for kids. It has all kinds of vitamins and minerals and is super gross, so I decided to experiment with liver instead of chicken.

I would try to find a way to change the awful taste of liver to the delicious taste of candy canes. The reason I chose candy canes was because my kid sister loves candy canes more than anyone I have ever met. Every year she can't wait until they are on sale, which is usually right after Halloween.

I deleted the part about chicken and changed it to liver. Then I continued typing.

Hypothesis: I think I can invent something that will change liver so it tastes like candy canes.

I knew this had to be more than an ingredient of some sort. It had to be something that actually changed the liver so much it didn't taste like liver at all.

This idea was perfect. All parents have trouble getting little kids to eat healthy food. The challenge would be to create a way to do more than just season food. This invention had to change the food so much that kids wouldn't be able to taste the difference.

Materials: Emma, a few pounds of liver, and something that will change the liver to taste like candy canes.

Procedure: I will change liver in a number of different ways in order to make it taste like candy canes. I will feed it to my sister and she will give me feedback on the liver's taste.

Results:

I couldn't do that yet because I didn't know what would happen.

I stopped typing. "Emma, tomorrow you are coming with me to the lab."

"I am? Promise?"

"I promise. The only rule is you can't tell anyone what my experiment is and you have to come with me and eat dinner right now."

I explained the idea to her, and she was all excited. She agreed to eat her dinner, and for the first time in who knows how long, my little sister went downstairs and ate her dinner. She looked like she might give up a few times. She said, "This is awful," about a hundred times, and she even cried at one point, but she ate it. Mom and Dad looked on in disbelief. When Emma was done she turned to me and said, "We have a deal."

"Yes," I said. "We have a deal."

"What are you two talking about?" Mom asked. "How in the world did you get Emma to finally eat? I am absolutely astonished! Emma, I am so proud of you! Keith, how did you do this?"

"Trust me, Mom," I said. "Just trust me."

CHAPTER 22

No Good Thing
Ever Is . . .

The next day Emma and I went right to the lab. We got there before anyone else. I didn't want anyone to know what I was working on with Emma. I arranged for Mr. Carson, one of the scientists from Mr. Gonzalez's lab, to pick us up early.

Once we got to the lab, I said, "Okay, Mr. Carson, I finally know what I'm going to do for my experiment."

"Nothing like waiting until the last minute," he said. "Mr. Gonzalez was starting to worry about you."

"I thought he was unable to be reached while he was away. You mean you've talked to him?"

"Of course. You think a man that important goes away and can't communicate? Do you understand how important he is, Keith?"

"I do. It's just that he told me he couldn't be reached."

"Couldn't be reached by *you*. He knew if you could reach him you would be calling him for help. He wanted this idea to come from you, like the last one did. Now what is the idea? We don't have a lot of time."

Emma and I spent the next hour explaining to him all about her difficulty eating food. I explained that I didn't want to simply season food. I wanted to change food so it tasted nothing like the way it normally tastes, but still retained all its nutritional value.

"I'm not sure I follow completely," he said.

I made it as clear as possible. "For example, let's say Emma was eating a piece of liver."

Emma made a face.

"I want the liver to change completely in texture, smell, and taste so that she would think she was eating a piece of candy cane."

For a good minute Mr. Carson looked at me and then said, "We could experiment with the molecular makeup of foods and try to alter it so that it gives the person eating one food the illusion of eating another." He paused and said, "Intriguing . . . You may be a great scientific mind after all, Keith. You are talking about molecular gastronomy. There are many famous chefs using this in fancy restaurants around the world right now. I don't know of anyone focusing on changing foods so children eat better. If you could solve the age-old problem of kids not wanting to eat their food, it would be quite a discovery. My kids won't eat anything but hot dogs and pizza without a struggle. This is not going to be easy, but no good thing ever is. Our biggest problem now is we only have one week until Mr. Gonzalez comes back."

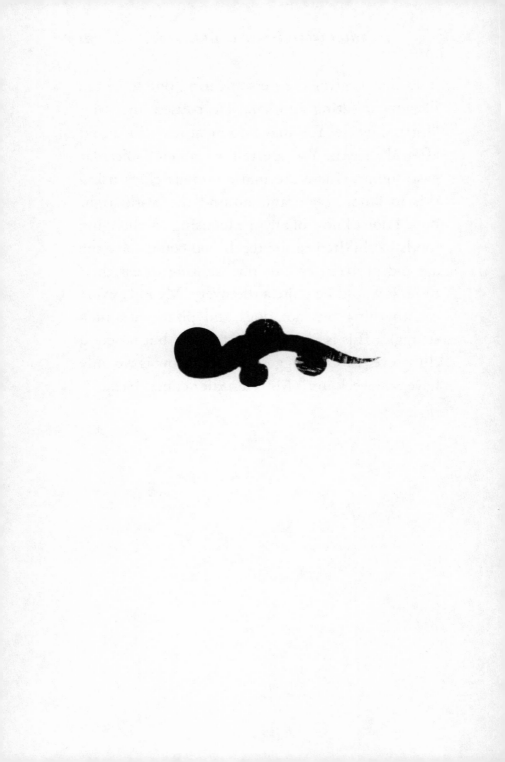

CHAPTER 23

The *Helen Winifred Show* Pre-Interview

The weekend before Mr. Gonzalez came back into town some people from *The Helen Winifred Show* came to shoot footage of our family at home, my school, and me in the lab.

Mom was a complete wreck all week. She went to the hair salon three different times, had a manicure, pedicure, the works. Emma also went with Mom and had her hair done up all fancy. They both got completely new outfits. Then Mom got an email from one of the show's producers saying that they wanted our family to dress and act like we normally do. They wanted to get an idea of what our family was like on an average weekend day.

Mom got triple worried after that email. "They want to see what we are like on a normal day? They want to see what we are like on a normal day? We are completely not normal on a normal day!" I heard her telling my dad in the kitchen as I finished up my dinner at the table.

"It will be fine," my dad told her. "Emma is eating again. Keith seems more calm about his experiment. *You have an idea right? Son?*" he shouted.

I got up from the table and went into the kitchen. "Yeah, and I think it's pretty good, too. I just don't know if there's enough time. The good news is that Emma will be helping me."

"What do you mean? How is Emma going to help you?" Mom asked.

"I don't want to give it away, but let's just say you are going to like it."

"If Emma keeps eating, I don't care what it is, I will like it."

"They're here! They're here!" Emma came running into the kitchen.

"Okay, everyone, please be as normal as possible. I'm sure these people are looking for any opportunity to make us look like crazy people," Mom said.

"It will be fine, Mom. Relax." *How come I'm the calm one,* I thought.

Emma ran up to the door. "Who is it?" she asked.

"Debbie Francis, the producer of *The Helen Winifred Show* in New York," a voice answered.

Emma opened the door and gave a long dramatic bow.

Debbie Francis said, "Oh my! Aren't you the cutest little thing?"

Emma curtsied and let one go so loud I thought Debbie Francis's eyes were going to leap out of her head. Behind her was a cameraman who was pointing his camera directly at Emma.

"Good afternoon and welcome to the house that Farts built," Emma announced. "Farts is my brother's nickname, but you can call him Gooz. That means *fart* in Farsi."

"Well, that was quite a welcome," Mrs. Francis replied, trying to keep from laughing. My dad grabbed Emma and carried her off somewhere else in the house.

"I'm so terribly sorry," my mom said. "Emma is not herself these days, what with the excitement of Keith inventing Sweet Farts and a TV crew coming to our house. Please forgive us." She turned to the cameraman. "Please erase that, I am begging you."

"Sorry, lady," he replied. "That sort of thing happens once in a lifetime. Helen Winifred is going to love it!"

"Oh dear," my mom said, turning a deep shade of pink.

"Relax, Mom," I whispered. I turned back to Mrs. Francis. "Hi, I'm Keith Emerson. Please come in. My mother is just having a mind melt. She'll be fine in a little while."

"Thank you," Mrs. Francis said. She came in and sat on the couch in the living room. The cameraman asked if he could walk around and videotape some of the house. I told him it was fine. Mom just sat on the couch next to me. It was as if she had gone into some kind of shock. She just smiled. She didn't say a word, just smiled. From Emma's room I could hear her saying, "What's the problem? Fawting is the family business!"

This interview is going to have to be all on me, I thought.

The preshow interview was pretty awkward. My mom said nothing, and Emma kept shouting about the family business. I think Mrs. Francis got the impression that it wasn't a good time, because after about a half hour she and the cameraman left. I told them I would catch up with them at the lab in a little while. They said thanks and headed off to visit the school and then the lab. I stayed home to help Mom snap out of it.

CHAPTER 24

Mr. Gonzalez Returns

The next week Mr. Gonzalez finally returned from his trip. When I arrived at the lab on Monday afternoon, he was in my room with Mr. Carson. When I walked in, they both stopped talking and turned to me.

"Hi, Keith. I was just talking with Mr. Carson, and I'm very interested in your idea. I think you are definitely on to something here with your molecular gastronomy project. I just wish you had thought of it sooner. Making any sort of progress is going to be really hard in just a week's time."

"I know," I said.

"I understand that you and Mr. Carson have worked very hard during the last week experimenting with different methods of altering liver to taste and smell like candy canes. We have arranged a little taste test to take place in a few minutes to see what kind of progress you have made. In the meantime, why don't you show me how you plan to record your results."

I sat down at my computer and pulled up the files I had been working on all week with Mr. Carson. "Okay," I said. "Just like I did with Sweet Farts, I am going to use a rubric to rate the taste of the food on a scale from 1 to 4."

Mr. Gonzalez read the rubric over my shoulder:

Candy Cane Liver Rubric:
4 = Liver tastes exactly like a candy cane.
3 = Liver tastes mostly like a candy cane but has some qualities of liver.
2 = Liver tastes slightly like a candy cane but has many qualities of liver.
1 = Liver tastes like liver. Not at all like a candy cane.

"All right, it seems like you have put some thought into this after all. Who do you plan to test?"

"I was thinking about testing my sister, since

she is the one who came up with the idea in the first place."

"Your little sister came up with this idea?" he asked, amazed.

"Yeah, I'm sorry. I know it was supposed to come from me. It's just that she was having such trouble eating food. She didn't want to eat anything and I was really starting to worry about her. So I figured that if I did this I could try to help her."

"Keith, there's nothing wrong with getting the idea from your sister. Scientists have to listen to the world around them if they hope to make inventions that people actually need and care about. I'm just amazed that such a young person came up with such an amazing idea."

"Yeah, well, my sister is something else."

"I hear that her class is something else as well, and if I'm not mistaken that is them pulling up right now." Through the window I could see a bus pulling into the lab parking lot. I looked at Mr. Carson.

"You don't have a lot of time. You need to gather data as quickly as possible. I suggested to Mr. Gonzalez that we invite Emma's class in for a taste test. Go print out about thirty copies of your rubric and grab a bunch of crayons from somewhere. These kids are going to be hungry."

"We aren't ready," I reminded him.

"Time waits for no man, Keith. This is going to be your first trial. You have to start somewhere. You know the fifty pieces of liver we altered last week? They're in the refrigerator. Go get them and bring them out. Let's see if the great Keith Emerson has done it again."

CHAPTER 25

A Classic

I walked out of the lab room with a large tray of what I hoped would be Candy Cane Liver and saw Emma and her entire class sitting at tables set up on the basketball court. They were so loud I couldn't believe it. Emma saw me and came running up to give me a hug. I had to put the tray of altered liver down on one of the tables.

"Hey, Emma, this is a surprise. Are you excited to try the liver I've been working on?"

"I sure am," she said enthusiastically. "I told my whole class that you had fixed food for evow."

"Well, Emma, I've only been working on this for about a week. I can't say if it is going to work or not."

Emma pointed her fingers at me as if shooting a gun and fired one off. "Emma, you really have to get your gas under control. Remember we talked about this. You can't pass gas like that at school."

"I don't want to control it," she said. "Today I took Pickle scent. It's a classic, Keith. Enjoy." Emma went back to her seat beaming.

I realized something about Emma's class that I wasn't quite prepared for. I realized it as soon as I started talking to them. As I walked around the court trying to keep their attention I smelled just about every Sweet Farts scent there was. These kids weren't holding back one bit. As I talked, several kids just let them go as loud as they pleased. It was nothing to them. I looked at Emma's teacher, and she just shrugged. "Thanks to Sweet Farts, these kids don't have any problem passing gas whenever they want. We try to stop them, but it just doesn't work," she told me over the noise.

Something hit me as I thought about that. Benjamin Franklin had said in 1781 that if someone could make the smell of human gas pleasant, passing gas would be no worse that sneezing. Looking out at this gassy bunch of kids I realized that he was right. These kids didn't know any better. They thought farts were fun and nothing to be embarrassed about. I wasn't sure how I felt about it, but they sure seemed happy.

"Keith!" Mr. Gonzalez pointed to the clock. "Let's get this going. These kids need to be home in about an hour."

Mr. Carson looked at me and shrugged. *Well, here goes nothing,* I thought.

"Hi, everyone."

"Hi, Farts," they answered in unison.

"My name is Keith. I am Emma's big brother. We have asked you here today because we are working on an invention that will turn the taste of any food you don't like into the taste of a food you do like." They all cheered.

A little boy at the back of the court raised his hand.

"Yes?"

"I hate peas," he announced.

"Okay," I replied. "And what else did you want to say?"

"That's it, I just hate peas."

"Oh, thanks for sharing that. Now . . ."

Every hand went up instantly. I picked a little girl in the front sitting next to my sister.

"I don't like steak," she announced.

"I'm sorry to hear that," I said. "I'm sure you

all have foods that you don't like to eat, and that's why I've tried to make this invention. Today we are going to eat some liver." The entire room let out a loud *"Eeewwwww!"*

"Most kids really dislike liver, so I thought it was the perfect food to test. My friend Mr. Carson and I are going to give you something that looks like liver, but if everything went well, it will taste like candy canes." I had really wanted to change the entire look of the food so it looked like a candy cane, but we hadn't made it that far yet. For now, the food looked the way it always looked, so the liver looked like liver. Mr. Carson and I walked around, giving each kid a plate with a piece of the altered liver on it. They all made faces and said it looked yucky.

I then held up the rubric and told them that after tasting the food they would give it a score from 1 to 4. I wasn't completely sure they understood me even though they all nodded as if they did. "I will count to three and then everyone will taste it. Here we go: One, two, three. Taste!" I shouted. No one picked up the fork. They all just looked at me.

Emma broke the silence. "It looks really gross."

"I know it looks gross, but it should taste great. Come on, trust us. Give it a try."

A really small kid in the middle of the group announced, "I'll do it."

"That's Ronnie," my sister interrupted. "He picks his nose and eats it."

"I do not!" Ronnie shouted back.

"You eat boogers!" Emma insisted.

"Wow!" I said. "Emma, that isn't very nice. You shouldn't say things like that about other people. I'm sorry, Ronnie. Will you go ahead and try it?"

Ronnie slowly picked up his fork. He pushed his fork down on his piece of liver, he slowly lifted the fork to his nose and took a sniff. He paused a good long pause. You could have heard a pin drop. All eyes were on Ronnie. He finally took a slow bite. The instant the liver hit his lips he spit it out, and it flew across the table and landed in a little girl's hair. She immediately stood up and started running across the basketball court, trying to get the liver out of her hair. The rest of the class exploded with sound as they all jumped out of their chairs and started running around the gym pretending to get food out of their hair.

I looked at Mr. Gonzalez from across the madness. He mouthed, *You have one week.* I exhaled a deep, long breath. This wasn't going to be easy.

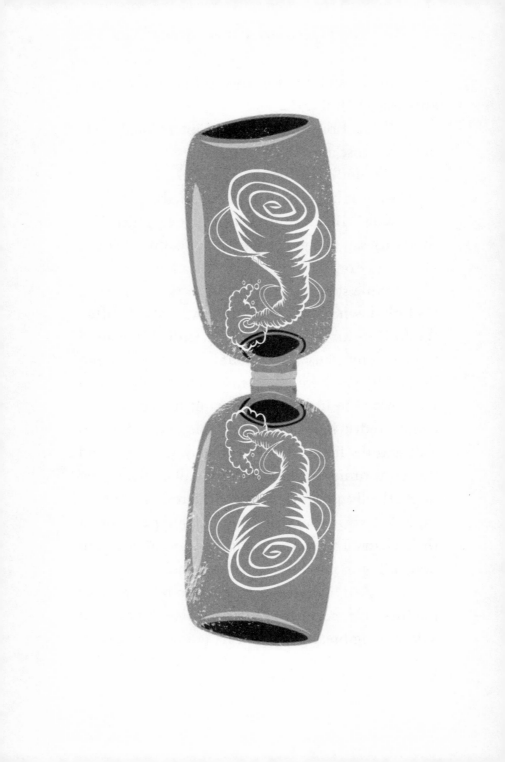

CHAPTER 26

Do You Love It?

The week leading up to the fair was not a pretty one. My sister decided about halfway through the week that she was not going to taste any of my science-fair food. She said it was so bad she would rather eat regular food, which she did. Mr. Carson and I worked late into the night every night that week. At school I felt like I wasn't even there.

We researched the many ways in which fancy chefs create amazing new flavors. We used equipment that measured the molecular structure of liver and candy canes. Mr. Carson had a whole bunch of strange cooking tools delivered, and we experimented with them hour after hour. I was sure we were close to perfecting Candy Cane Liver a few times, but we just couldn't seem to get it right.

No matter what we did I could still taste liver.

The hardest part was that the science was so challenging for me. I didn't have enough education to really take on such a complicated experiment, but it was what my sister wanted, so I tried.

The day of the fair was pretty bad. Mr. Michaels had designated a special spot for me to display my project right at the entrance to the school. There was a banner behind me that had a huge picture of me holding a pack of Sweet Farts. It read, "Harborside's Own Keith Emerson, Inventor of the Internationally Best-Selling Sweet Farts!" Then it listed the whole story of how I invented Sweet Farts.

I was completely exhausted. I had worked all through the night. I think I fell asleep in a chair at one point, but I couldn't remember clearly. I had eaten a whole lot of liver, I knew that.

My booth was completely packed at the beginning of the fair, but it got quiet really fast as people realized all I had was an idea and no actual invention to talk about. I displayed a few pieces of the different versions of Candy Cane Liver we had prepared. One kid tried it and spit it out. "Your project is gross," he assured me.

A few booths down the hall was Anthony's project. He seemed to be packed all day long. I was amazed at how much work he had done. He had graphs, charts, and a huge computer screen with pictures of him at work in the lab. He was going on and on about his theories and the patterns he claimed to have discovered in the lottery numbers. That kid sure can talk. I watched him as he went on and on about how he was pretty sure he would win the lottery soon.

All of a sudden I realized that I hadn't seen Scott. I decided to walk around and find him. He had been really secretive about his experiment ever since he and Anthony had split up. I walked all around the school and finally found him set up in our classroom. He was nowhere to be found, but on his desk was his experiment. It was a couple of two-liter soda bottles, one on top of the other. They were attached at the openings with tape, and one was half-filled with colored water. I couldn't believe it. He had done the classic lazy man's science experiment. He had done the tornado in a bottle!

"Do you love it?" he asked from behind me.

"You can't be serious with this. I'm going absolutely nuts for the past two months and you do a tornado in a bottle? How long did this take you?"

"Cranked it out this morning," he said proudly. "I had to have my mom help me hold it while I taped it together."

"What have you been doing for the past couple of weeks?"

"I hired a hitting coach. He's been working on my swing with me on the pitching machine at the lab. I am going to crush the ball this spring."

CHAPTER 27

The Helen Winifred Show

After the fair we all piled into a big car that Mr. Gonzalez had sent. He was sitting inside when we were picked up. "Well, how did it go?" he asked.

"You know how it went. I had all these people counting on me, and I let them down. It was a total embarrassment."

"Oh, that's nothing, Keith. You had amazing success with Sweet Farts. You're a scientist now. You need to realize that failure is part of being a scientist. Do you know that I have failed far more than I have succeeded? You will fail, but you cannot quit. At least you know now what not to do as you move forward with your research."

"What do you mean move forward? The science fair is over."

"The science fair may be over, but the science is not. You have great ideas, and you owe it to yourself, to your family, to me, and to Benjamin Franklin to keep working on them."

I took a deep breath. "I thought for sure you were going to kick me out of the lab."

"No, Keith, the lab is yours. You and your friends are free to use that space as you see fit. In a way, you are an experiment of mine. I see something in you. You choose to surround yourself with your friends and your family. I have to believe in that and see where it takes you." Then he turned and looked at Scott. "If, however, you pull a stunt like that next year, you will be out. Do you understand, Scott?"

"Yes, Mr. Gonzalez," Scott said, nodding.

During the drive to *The Helen Winifred Show* I felt both worried and relieved—worried because I was about to go on TV and explain how I had failed in my science experiment, and relieved that the fair was over. It had been a tough few weeks. I was happy to sit and just look out the window.

When we finally arrived in New York City, I sat backstage at *The Helen Winifred Show,* waiting for my turn to go on. I couldn't help but think it shouldn't be me out there on the stage. I had nothing to really talk about. My experiment was a flop.

Just then, a woman wearing a headset and holding a clipboard walked into the room and signaled that it was time for me to go on. I felt my chest tighten. All of a sudden I was aware of my breathing. When I stood up, I felt a little dizzy, and my stomach filled with butterflies.

I followed her down a long hallway lined with pictures of all the famous people Helen Winifred had interviewed. The hallway seemed to go on forever, and I half wished it would, so I would never make it to the stage. At the end of the hall we reached a door. A blinking light at the top of the door read "Live."

My mom had watched Helen Winifred practically every day of my entire life, and I had never stopped to think about the fact that it was not taped but live. Suddenly, however, I realized that if I made a mistake or did something embarrassing, it was going out live to the whole world.

The lady with the headset opened the door and signaled for me to follow. I heard the energy of the crowd. It was really loud. Then I heard Helen Winifred's voice: "My next guest is a ten-year-old boy from Long Island, New York. Last school year he made an invention that changed the world."

The woman with the headset held up her hand, signaling for me to stop. I could see Helen Winifred through a curtain in front of me. I could also see the crowd of moms listening to her every word. "My grandmother used to say, 'If you think something stinks in life, fix it!'" she said. "Well, my grandmother would have been very proud of this young man because that is exactly what he did. Please welcome Keith Emerson, inventor of Sweet Farts!"

The crowd clapped, and I could hear Anthony and Scott whistling and hooting as if they were at a football game. They were seated right in the front row, along with my mom and dad, Emma, Grandma, and Mr. Gonzalez.

I shook Helen's hand and sat in the big comfy chair next to hers. "Hey, Keith," Helen said.

"Hey to you," I replied, nervously.

"I have heard of some pretty good nicknames in my day, but I heard you have a few that just might take the cake."

I couldn't believe this. Was she really going to talk about my nicknames in public?

"Now, I'm going to apologize up front for what we are going to do. I hope you are a good sport about it. We asked your mom, and she said you would be okay." I looked at my mom and she responded with a sinister smile. *Oh, no,* I thought. *She's about to get back at me for all the embarrassment I put her through when I invented Sweet Farts.*

Just then the lights dimmed and game-show music came on. Helen said, "We are going to play a little game with the audience. Each person has an electronic device that will allow them to answer multiple-choice questions *A, B, C,* or *D.* I will ask the questions, they will select their answer, and the data will be immediately displayed on the screen behind us. Are you ready?"

I was in shock. Was this really happening? Had my life just become a complete joke to everyone? And why was Mom allowing this? Grandma shouted above the crowd, "Let's play!"

Helen started laughing. "That's your grandma, right?"

"Yup," I said, defeated.

"Well, you heard the woman. Let's play what's Keith's nickname!" The music swelled and then fell silent as Helen read from the cards in her hands. "Was Keith's nickname at school last year (a) Dust, (b) S.B.D., Silent But Deadly, (c) The Punisher, or (d) Air Poo.

The audience giggled like crazy and looked down at their electronic devices. The data was immediately displayed on the screen behind Helen and me. Helen read the results. "Sixty-three percent picked Air Poo, 37 percent picked S.B.D., 8 percent picked The Punisher, and only 2 percent picked Dust." The crowd cheered.

I must have looked really uncomfortable in my chair, because Helen asked, "Are you okay? I'm sorry, I can tell this is really bothering you. We were just trying to have a little fun. Your friends told us you would get a kick out of this."

"I'm fine," I said. "I'm kind of used to it. My friends have a habit of putting me in embarrassing situations."

"I've heard a lot about these nicknames. What's the story behind them? Which one is the correct nickname from the game?"

"Well, they used to call me S.B.D." The crowd went crazy.

"Everyone who guessed S.B.D. will be taking home a year's supply of Sweet Farts," Helen announced. The women all let out an ear-piercing shriek of approval.

I waited until they quieted down, and then continued. "They called me S.B.D. for Silent But

Deadly because everyone thought I was farting in class, even though it was never once me. From there it grew into Sweet Farts, and then they started calling me just plain Farts. Most recently, their favorite is Gooz, the Farsi word for *fart*."

Helen was trying not to laugh, but she couldn't hold it in. "That's awful . . . for you . . . and really funny for us. Those are some tough nicknames to deal with. May I call you Gooz? Because I really like that name, but I understand if you don't like it."

"Go ahead, enjoy it." I said. The crowd cheered again, and for the first time in a long time I felt relaxed, on live television, of all places.

"So moving off the fart focus for a minute, what was your project this year? I know there were a lot of expectations and excitement about what you would invent next. Did you fix the smell of vomit, because a lot of people thought that was your next idea."

I looked at my family and smiled. "No, we thought about doing that, but decided against it after an unfortunate event in the lab." I looked at my dad, and he was gagging a little and covering his mouth.

"Okay, so what did you do?"

"Well, Helen, I set out to find a cure for kids

who hate to eat healthy food. My sister wouldn't eat, so I tried to invent a way to make yucky foods taste like something yummy. So if a kid were eating liver, for example, when she tasted it she would taste another food, such as candy canes, but get the nutrition of the liver."

"Wow, that's pretty cool. How did it turn out?"

"I couldn't do it. I failed." The crowd let out a long "*Aaawww.*"

"Well, don't say that," Helen encouraged. "There aren't too many ten-year-olds who can say they have an invention like Sweet Farts selling around the world and their very own lab to work in." The crowd cheered and clapped for me. It felt pretty good, but I couldn't help feeling that I had let everyone down.

"I hear you have your own company. What's the name of it, and who are your employees?"

"Well, our name is—" I looked at my family and the name just came to me: "Sweet Farts Incorporated, and the employees are me, my dad, my friends Scott and Anthony, and my grandma." Grandma let out a loud "Yeah!" for some reason. "And I am proud to announce our newest employee, my little sister, Emma. Without her I would have had no idea for an experiment this year. Go ahead and stand up, Emma," I told her.

Again the crowd went, *"Aaawwww."*

Emma stood up. "Really?" she asked over the applause.

"Yes," I said. "You have earned it, Emma. You are officially in the family business." It was nice to see Emma so proud of herself.

Just then, Anthony climbed up on his seat, held up his cell phone, and shouted, "I did it! I did it!"

"Anthony!" I burst out. "We are on live TV here."

"I know, but I just beat the lottery! I won 178 million dollars. I'm rich, man! Rich, I tell ya!" He hugged Scott, and they both jumped up and down on their chairs.

"Who is this person?" Helen interrupted.

"This is my friend Anthony. His experiment was to try and find patterns in the lottery." I turned to Anthony. "Come on, Anthony. Stop fooling around."

"I just got an email with the winning numbers. I won, baby! You're looking at a genius," he shouted. The crowd went absolutely nuts.

"Well, Gooz," Helen said over the cheers, "it looks like your company is doing something right."

"I guess we are," I said. "I guess we are."

CHAPTER 28

The Thank-You

After the show we were all sitting backstage and Helen Winifred came into my room to say goodbye.

"You were a good sport out there, Keith. I think what you guys are doing is pretty amazing. I wish Sweet Farts Inc. all the luck in the future." She turned to Anthony. "Congratulations on your lottery winning. I think that is amazing. Next year we will have to invite you both back to discuss your science projects." Then she turned to Mom. "I would like to thank you for putting up with your son while he invented Sweet Farts. I give them to my dog, and let's just say, it's necessary."

She took a picture with all of us and said goodbye. Then we all started walking down the hallway toward the street. We walked right past

Helen Winifred's dressing room. I noticed that Grandma was hanging far back from the rest of us. As she passed Helen's dressing room, she ducked in for a moment and then came back out.

When we got in the car, Grandma sat next to me. "I am so proud of you, Keith. You were such a gentleman in there. I think you should feel pretty great about yourself right now."

"Thanks, Grandma. I noticed you snuck into Helen's dressing room on the way out. What was that all about?"

"Oh, I just wanted to drop a little thank-you on her desk, that's all."

CHAPTER 29

In the End

That night we all went to the lab. We ordered a bunch of pizzas and just hung out. Scott and Anthony were playing basketball in their fancy clothes. Mr. Gonzalez and Mr. Carson were talking at a table and having a cup of coffee. Emma was asleep on one of the couches. Grandma was in the kitchen doing something.

I was sitting on the couch across from Emma with my mom seated on one side of me and my dad on the other.

"You handled yourself really well today, Keith," Mom said.

"Yeah, I have to give you credit, son. You've dealt with a lot over the past few months. I don't know that I could have done it."

"Thanks, Dad. I appreciate it."

"No problem, son," he said. Then Dad leaned to his left side and let one go—it was the loudest and longest fart I have ever heard. It went on and on and got louder and louder. Just when I thought it was going to end, it kept going for what seemed an eternity. Emma woke from her sleep in terror; Anthony and Scott stopped in their tracks: Mr. Gonzalez and Mr. Carson both looked stunned. When it finally stopped the room was completely silent. Dad looked as proud as a peacock and announced, "I give you the amplifier, ladies and gentlemen." He stood up and was taking a bow.

"Awesome!" Anthony shouted from the basketball court.

"Honey, that was wrong on so many levels," Mom said as she walked to the other side of the room. "That is what you have been spending all your spare time on the past few months?"

"I want an amplifier," Emma pouted.

"Maybe for your birthday, sweetie," my dad said, amused.

Just then, Grandma walked in as if nothing had happened. She was holding a box that she set down on one of the tables. She started taking out green and orange squares and stacking them on the table.

"Grandma, you didn't!" I exclaimed.

"Oh, yes I did, Goozer my boy. Oh, yes I did!"

As I sat there on the couch sandwiched between my mother and my father taking a bite out of my first square pear, I realized something. First, I loved square pears.

"Awesome, Grandma!" I said. She just winked as she peeled a square orange.

Second, the people that had been frustrating me for the past two months were the same people I was most thankful for in that moment. Sure, Scott and Anthony made me crazy and gave me a hard time, but I don't know what I would do without them. They are ridiculous, but everyone needs a little ridiculous in their life.

Grandma is in her own world, there's no denying that, but she is so supportive of me. It doesn't matter what I am doing or thinking, she thinks it's the best. I'm lucky to have her.

In terms of Emma, Emma is still just a baby. If anything, I owed her an apology for creating all this Sweet Farts craziness when she was so young. I was pretty much responsible for turning her into a fart monster. I could only hope that as we grew older she would learn to use the lab for something she loved.

And my parents, well, my parents are the best. Do they drive me crazy sometimes? Sure! Do they give me a hard time? You bet. But at the end of the day, they want me to do well, and they are on my side, no matter what happens. Seriously, how many moms would allow their kid to experiment with farts?

In the end, the only one who didn't make some sort of great invention this year, besides Scott, was me.

Grandma's square fruit ended up taking supermarkets across the country by storm, especially after they were featured on *The Helen Winifred Show*. It turned out that the thank-you Grandma left on Helen's desk was a square pear and her cell phone number.

Anthony ended up building an extension to our space at the lab. He put in a private swimming pool, which, as far as I can tell, he uses strictly for cannonballs. Surprisingly, he also donated 20 percent of his money to the charity of my choice. I was shocked that Anthony was capable of such kindness. The more I get to know that guy the more surprising he becomes. They say "Never judge a book by its cover," and Anthony has certainly taught me that the saying is true. Who would have thought that gasbag would turn out to be a math genius?

It turns out he's pretty amazing on the computer as well. He created the company website www.sweetfartsinc.com so the kids at school will stop bugging us about what projects we are working on. Thanks to Anthony, we just post updates on the Web when we are working on something new.

As if that isn't enough, he helped the lotto people understand the patterns he had found. They decided to add letters to the lottery drawings as well as the numbers. Anthony felt it would make it more difficult for people to find patterns as he was able to do.

Emma continued to eat even though I haven't found a way to change liver to candy canes. Every day she reminds me that we have a deal, and every day I go to the lab and try my best to make good on my promise.

It was kind of amazing to think how much Sweet Farts Inc. had accomplished. We were even featured in a national science magazine as the most unexpected scientific company of the year. I guess a company like ours was pretty unique. I remember thinking that I was the only one who had a clue in this group of misfits. In the end, the one without a clue was me. I thought my company was made up of a bunch of lemons, but when I put those lemons together, I got lemonade. The saying still holds true: if life gives you lemons, make lemonade.

Lemons and lemonade, my friends, lemons and lemonade.

Acknowledgments

My wife Stacy calls the *Sweet Farts* books "smart books with silly titles." I love her description because it captures what I hoped to create. I'm very fortunate that she not only tolerates my writing, but *gets* my writing. It's not every wife who supports her husband writing books about farting! Stacy, thank you for your never-ending support and amazing sense of humor.

A HUGE thanks to my kids, Ethan and Chloe, who remind me every day how fun it is to be a kid.

Thanks to my brother, Paul, for being there every step of the way in my writing career with advice and feedback. Thanks to Mapleton Hill Media for helping me in so many ways with all things tech. Thanks to my mother for her ridiculously high level of enthusiasm for my books. You are very cute. Thanks to Pete and Pat for all their support.

Thanks to everyone at Booksurge, now Createspace, for your support and help in creating the first *Sweet Farts* book. You all exceeded my expectations at every step of the self-publishing process. Special thanks to: Jenny Legun, Tara Schuley, Thom Kephart, Laura Bonam, and Abby Harris. To anyone reading this who is thinking of self-publishing, get in touch with Createspace now! You will be glad you did.

Thanks to Jeff Bezos for creating a path for self-published authors to find a larger audience. Thanks to the amazing people at AmazonEncore, especially Alex Carr, who shared and trusted my vision for a second *Sweet Farts* book. He plucked me out of the many self-published books out there, and I'm grateful. Thank you to Sarah Tomashek, Sarah Gelman, and Vicky Griffith for everything you've done to help bring *Rippin' It Old-School* to young readers. Thank you to Rhalee Hughes for helping raise awareness and interest in the *Sweet Farts* series. Rhalee completely understood that I was trying to reach reluctant readers in a way that would entertain readers and gain support from teachers and parents.

Thanks to Taryn Fagerness for taking on an unknown author and sending his book across the pond. Taryn, thanks for believing in the books from the very beginning and helping *Sweet Farts* reach readers around the world.

Thanks to Tim Ditlow of Brilliance Audio for his interest in the *Sweet Farts* books. I can't wait to hear the audio versions.

Thanks to the many teachers, readers, and parents who have sent me emails and written reviews in support of the *Sweet Farts* books. Finally, thanks to every student who ever said to me, "I can't find anything to read that I like." I always dreamed of being a writer when I was a kid. Thanks for inspiring me to make that dream a reality. Lemons and lemonade, my friends, lemons and lemonade.

ABOUT THE AUTHOR

Raymond Bean is a fourth-grade teacher with a love for teaching, reading, and writing and holds a master's in Elementary Education. He is a fan of all things ridiculous. More than ten years of teaching have taught him that kids love books that make them laugh, teachers love books that have worthwhile content, and farts can be very funny. He wrote *Sweet Farts,* his first novel, to reach the most reluctant readers. He sold more than 11,000 copies (self-published) on his own before Amazon took notice. Soon after, AmazonEncore chose *Sweet Farts: Rippin' It Old-School* as its first title for its children's list. Raymond likes spending time with his family, fishing, writing, and laughing as much as possible. Born in Queens, New York, he has also lived in Los Angeles and San Diego, California. Currently, he lives with his wife, eight-year-old son, and four-year-old daughter on Long Island, New York.